Kathleen O Meara

Henri Perreyve and his counsels to the sick

Kathleen O Meara

Henri Perreyve and his counsels to the sick

ISBN/EAN: 9783742828798

Manufactured in Europe, USA, Canada, Australia, Japa

Cover: Foto ©Andreas Hilbeck / pixelio.de

Manufactured and distributed by brebook publishing software
(www.brebook.com)

Kathleen O Meara

Henri Perreyve and his counsels to the sick

HENRI PERREYVE

AND

HIS COUNSELS TO THE SICK

HENRI PERREYVE

AND

HIS COUNSELS TO THE SICK

BY

KATHLEEN O'MEARA

AUTHOR OF

"LIFE OF FREDERIC OZANAM," "THOMAS GRANT, FIRST BISHOP
OF SOUTHWARK," "BELLS OF THE SANCTUARY," ETC.

LONDON

C. KEGAN PAUL & CO., 1, PATERNOSTER SQUARE

1881

PREFACE.

———◦◦◦———

I HAVE translated Henri Perreyve's "Journée des
Malades" at the earnest request of one who owes
the book a debt of gratitude, which it seemed to
him he might in part repay by passing on to others
the consolation he had himself found in its companionship during a long and painful illness.

The book needs no comment of mine. "All
that is written here, was suffered before it was
written," Henri Perreyve says in offering us this
sursum corda of a Christian on the Cross. This is
what constitutes its power, and explains the extraordinary grace and strength of consolation
which so many find in its pages. It is a record of
personal experience, and the outcome of a life
which combined with singular perfection the three

services—working, waiting, and suffering. It is not merely a message full of the unction of resignation to those stricken with actual illness; it is a lesson full of encouragement to many besides.

Those who are not already acquainted with Henri Perreyve will, I hope, be interested in the short sketch * of his life which I have prefixed to the translation of the "Journée des Malades." It was a pure and faithful life, fruitful in beautiful works, although it was so short: but its chief mission seems to me to have been to *live* this book; to show how it is possible for the will, when stimulated by faith and love, to lift the body above weak and suffering nature, and to rise, in spite of chronic ill health, to the generous and persevering effort of regular work. I trust and believe that this legacy of Henri Perreyve's, which is here presented to his English fellow-sufferers, will prove a solace to many of them, and cheer some of those hours that hang so heavily in a sick-room.

This sketch originally appeared in the "Ave Maria" of Indiana.

CONTENTS.

———◦◇◦———

Contents.

HENRI PERREYVE.

—◦◦◦—

THERE is nothing so wonderful as the variety of God's works in nature, unless it be the diversity of His likeness in souls. Sanctity, while it faithfully adheres to the essential lines of the Divine Model, reveals itself by characteristics as distinctive and manifold as the features of the human face, or the leaves of the forest; and just as star differeth from star in brightness, without the variety of their splendour disturbing the music of the spheres, or as one voice in a well-ordered choir will rise in sweet predominance above the rest without marring the harmony of the whole, so does one conspicuous virtue, one divine characteristic, strike as it were the key-note of the soul where all are singing in unison. The key-note of Henri Perreyve's soul was his love of beauty. It drew him to God like a magnet; to that Beauty, ever ancient and ever new, of which he would seem to have been born enamoured. On the day of his First Com-

munion it revealed itself to his young heart with the
clearness of a vision, enshrining itself in his soul for ever
after, to the exclusion of all earthly loves. On that
memorable morning, kneeling on the red velvet *prie-dieu*
in the old church of St Sulpice, Henri heard the voice
of the Beautiful One calling him to His service, and he
answered unhesitatingly, "Lord, I come!" But, though
he never wavered in his allegiance to that divine call, his
vocation was to be put to a long test before he finally
embraced it.

The Perreyve family were of Lyonnese origin. Henri
was born in Paris (April 11th, 1831), but a great part of
his childhood was spent in the old home at Lyons, where
his grandfather continued to reside after his son had
gone to Paris and started in the practice of the law.
M. Perreyve, Henri's father, was a distinguished Latinist,
as well as an able jurisconsult, and he intended his son
to adopt the bar as a profession. Out of deference to
the wishes of his parents, the boy followed the classes of
the Lycée St. Louis, and then entered on a course of law
at home, working hard at the study of philosophy at
the same time. Just as he reached his seventeenth
year, the Revolution broke out (1848), and the peaceful life of the young student was for a moment swept
into the current of national excitement. Monsieur
Perreyve, sharing the patriotic enthusiasm that moved
the worthiest of his fellow-citizens, enrolled himself in
the National Guard and went out to his duty in the

streets of Paris; and Henri insisted on shouldering a
musket and accompanying him, in spite of his mother's
fears and expostulations. He relates the result himself
in a letter dated July 7th, 1848: " My father and I were
on duty every day, and even every night, of the insurrec-
tion, without getting a single wound. Yet it was not for
lack of opportunities. Every moment we saw soldiers
of the line and *Gardes Mobiles* falling around us. . . .
M. Barch told me he was quite put out at coming home
without some honourable scar! No doubt, if one might
guide the ball oneself, a wound after such a fight would
be very precious. But, if we got off safe, Paris has
suffered terribly. There was nothing to be seen last
week but funerals. Yesterday the public ceremony took
place. An immense altar, draped in black and silver,
supported by high pillars and surmounted by a veiled
cross, was erected in the Place de la Concorde. All
the great bodies of the state, several regiments, legions
of the National Guard, covered the vast square, and
the deep silence and recollection were only broken by
the muffled roll of the drums and the solemn chants of
a large orchestra. The sun shone out magnificently;
the day was splendid. At the elevation of the Host, the
entire multitude knelt, the drums beat, all the bells of
the city rang their peals; it was a sublime spectacle.
We must admit that if our metropolis is terrible to behold in the day of its wreck, it is great and beautiful on
the day of victory and triumph. . . . To-day the funeral

of Monseigneur Affre takes place. . . . Does not God
mean, by that awful blow, to awake our country from
the lethargy in which she has slept so long? M. de
Lamartine says that a nation should not regret the blood
it sheds in order to make eternal truths blossom forth !
You see, I take our epoch very philosophically, thereby
anticipating a little on the lectures I am to give next
year. If they should see fit to refuse me the right to
teach philosophy this year, I will always have religion—
that better philosophy—to fall back on."

Meantime, he began to teach "the better philosophy"
to a gathering of poor children in one of the worst
quarters of Paris. A group of young men had joined
together for the purpose of instructing these young pariahs
in the elementary sciences, and their religious instruction
devolved on Henri. His health, always delicate, was
not equal to the strain this work put upon it. He burst
a blood-vessel, and for the next year his life was in
danger ; all study was suspended, and he was condemned
to practice the philosophy he had hoped to teach, thus
graduating in the school which alone can lead to the
highest kind of success. He was ordered to Italy, a
banishment in which he was to find many compensations
for the interruption of his studies. His feelings on first
entering Rome were almost too deep for expression.
Here he beheld strength everywhere triumphant in
beauty, even amidst decay, the ruins of the past grander
in their cyclopean fragments than the mightiest effort of

the present. "Time, time ! it is here that one learns to recognize this terrible power," exclaims the traveller; . . . "everything testifies to its resistless force. . . . Yet, owing to a providence, which has, no doubt, its philosophical reason, the efforts of the mighty enemy seem to have no power against the relics of the old Roman world : these ruins are eternal, and cannot be destroyed.

"It is because of the great lesson which they teach humanity. God has set them side by side with the radiant̄monuments of the true religion, in order that we may by constant comparison choose between what is dead and what lives with an imperishable life. The Roman world is incredible in its grandeur; it is almost the idea of the Infinite, which a pagan people, not being able to conceive as an immaterial Being, strove to embody here below. One is struck by the idea of power and strength which prevails in the construction of public edifices."

But Rome had far deeper attractions for him than these noble ruins, which spoke more to his imagination than to his soul. His heart was with his treasure, and that was in the sanctuary. No delight in the beauty of this world, of art or nature, could draw away his mind from that first and supreme object of his life, the priesthood. He had broken the matter to his father, who received the appeal reverently, exacting, however, that Henri should pass his examinations for the law, which would involve a year's delay. Whilst he was in Rome he received the news of one of his young friends, Adolphe Perraud,* having decided on becoming a priest, and he thus writes to congratulate him :—

"I cannot remain silent. . . . I must embrace you as a brother in Jesus Christ ; that is, with all conceivable tenderness. . . . Courage, blessed friend ! courage ! You carry our vocation in yours ! We congratulate you for being the first to reach the goal. We give you joy; we follow you with pride ; for, again I say, your victory is ours, and we shall be saved with you. You may tremble, you may be sorrowful unto death, you may even weep in the solitude of your heart. It is ever so, and the combat between God and man is not a thing of yester-day. But don't take these things for hesitation. I am certain you do not hesitate. . . . Take courage; gird yourself with strength, and do not mistake for doubt and uncertainty the weakness of a heart overcome by its own glory, and sinking beneath the weight of its happiness. Our kings wept on the day of their coronation. On taking your first step in the 'Royal Highway' it is natural that you should feel the same emotion in your soul. Go forth ! Our pride and joy should reassure you. We salute you from afar, and pray God to give you strength interiorly to bear the burden of so great an honour."

With such bold and glowing wisdom did Henri cheer on his friends to the service of the sanctuary. If this should

---

* Afterwards Père Perraud, of the Oratory.

be a surprise to some, let them remember that in his eyes this vocation was not alone the most sublime prerogative, but the greatest joy—humanly and divinely—that God could bestow upon a soul. The world expresses no surprise when a young artist or a young soldier endeavours to win over his friends to the camp or the studio, and represents the career of his choice as the most delightful that a man can embrace; it has a smile of indulgence for the rash enthusiasm which exaggerates the glories of war and the delights of art, ignoring, with a treachery that is partly unconscious, the hardships, humiliations, and deceptions with which the road of each is strewn; but if a soldier of the Cross endeavours to recruit a comrade to the service of the Divine Master, this same world is scandalized at his imprudence, and loudly condemns his ill-advised zeal. Yet may we not all say with Père Gratry, "I know of no wiser enthusiasm than that which excites men to become the workmen of God!"

On the Tombs of the Apostles, Henri made a vow to renounce all that we call happiness, tranquillity, the interests of this world, in order to embrace a life of toil and struggle. "Shall I have strength to do it?" he exclaims. "I hope so, for I have rested my hopes in God alone." Writing to a friend who hesitated about entering the religious life, he says: "I dwell rather much on this point, that you may find happiness, real happiness, in the religious state; because it seems to me that

D——'s letter rather exaggerates the austere and sad side of such a resolution. The love of God is to me far more the *expression of life than the expression of death.*"

On his return from Italy, Henri made the acquaintance of Père Lacordaire. He had followed the conferences of the illustrious orator at Notre Dame, and conceived for his genius that passionate admiration which it awoke in the noblest minds of the age. This excess of admiration, however, inspired the young man with a certain awe, which made him fly from the great Dominican when he met him out of the pulpit. One day, a friend, who sometimes rallied him on the point, carried him off to see Père Lacordaire in his convent, Rue Vangirard. There were visitors in the room, and Père Lacordaire, who was very busy, divided between all the few moments he had to give; and, as Henri had no questions to ask, no notice was taken of him, and he left the room without having exchanged a word with the great man. But Lacordaire had seen him, and with that unerring instinct which enabled him to recognize at once "one of God's conquests," he read the beauty of the young man's soul upon his face. A few days later Henri was at work in his room, when there was a knock at his door, and Père Lacordaire walked in.

"*Mon enfant!*" he said, holding out his hand, "I received you badly the other day. I have come to beg your pardon, and to have a chat with you."

Thus did the great master, who was to give him so

many noble lessons, begin by giving him one of humility
and kindness. Few men possessed in a higher degree
than Père Lacordaire that *seeing* eye which discerns the
true ideal and detects the least flaw in its perfection.
In these first days of their intercourse, he pointed out
to Henri the mistake he made in separating beauty from
goodness, a divorce which he declared was absolutely
fatal to the former.

" Take a face," he said to him, "·where the regularity
of the lines and the softness of the contours are perfect,
but without any expression of goodness in the eyes, or
on the lips, and you will have the head of a Medusa."

Henri took the lesson to heart, and grew, says Père
Gratry, " in goodness and beauty, before God and man,
to the last day of his life."

But death was the teacher, above all others, which
sounded the *sursum corda !* that kept his eyes uplifted
to the eternal Beauty, towards which he was fast journey-
ing. The thought that he might soon be called away
from amidst men, inclined his heart to a tender indulgence
which is seldom the characteristic of holiness in the
young. "The habit of being dangerously ill," he says
himself, "has inclined me to love men. I feel that, as
life is short, we ought not to waste it in hating each
other; and as death is at our heels, we ought all to be
ready to leave the world on friendly terms."

The grim professor kept faithful watch by him. His
health, which had improved during his visit to Italy,

again alarmed his family, and he was obliged to spend
the winter at Pau. He worked hard to make up for
lost time in view of the approaching examinations, and
found in the beauty of nature some compensation for
the absence of friends.

"The weather is superb, the mountains more beautiful
on account of the snow, the torrents are white with foam,
the pastures green and rich with herds and flocks; the
mountaineers are swift-footed, the songs from the valley
are plaintive, the solitary hours full of memories, and
I am always your friend."

Early in January (1852) he went up for his examina-
tion at Toulouse, and announced the results to his parents
on the 19th. "I don't wait to doff my cap and gown
to embrace you. . . . I have had almost a success. . . .
I held forth à la méridionale, and, with God's help, came
pretty well out of it."

This was a modest report of an ordeal which won for
the competitor the applause of all present, and flattering
congratulations from the examiners.

While Henri was quietly engaged in these intellectual
combats, France was passing through a crisis from which
the ardent heart of the young student could not hold
aloof in indifference. The *Coup d'Etat*, so variously
judged by opposing parties, had sent a thrill of horror
through the country, and many who had hailed the
advent of Napoleon III. as that of the heaven-sent
minister who was to rescue the nation from anarchy, now

recoiled in dismay, their confidence shaken, or changed to indignation and hostility.

"It seems to me," writes Henri, "that liberty is dead in our unfortunate France. Too much applause, too many hurrahs greeted everywhere, what I must call the violation of our fatherland. I feel as if there were nothing to do, nothing to hope for; shame and humiliation arc all that remain to us in such depths of degradation. We must seek a Master and a fatherland above, and no longer waste our hopes on a phantom who has proved false to himself."

Henri formed one of that aspiring band who called Ozanam their leader, and who, having lost all confidence in the old monarchical rule, looked for the salvation of France to the reign of free democracy as it exists in America. The violence which ushered in the empire did not tend to check their admiration for the republican form of government.

"What is to be done?" exclaims Henri. "What I believed before, I believe still—if the happiness of humanity is in the application of the widest democratic system, the democratic system is only possible on condition of being founded upon Christian virtues. We are not Christians, consequently we shall be slaves. That is all."

He continued faithful to his principle of democracy when many of his friends had rallied to the Empire, now surrounded with the prestige of success, and about to enter on the brilliant military phase of its career. "I should like to know what you think of this war (the Crimean)," he writes to the Père Lacordaire; " it seems to me that it is a fine war. But how much finer it would be if it were undertaken in the name of democracy! As it is, it must inevitably be the triumph of egotism and tyranny. And yet that odious Russian Empire is so near Constantinople, and Constantinople is so near Rome, that from the catholic point of view the question seems to me of appalling gravity. Does not the prophecy of Napoleon I. appear astounding?—'France will be Republican or Cossack.' How many Frenchmen are likely to perish for not having believed in these words! But there is no enthusiasm! Everything is so dead! I am not yet very old, and yet what hours and days I spent crying out to M. de Lamartine under the balconies of the Hôtel de Ville—'War for Poland! The deliverance of Poland!' There was life in those days anyhow; but now . . ."

Even to the last, when life was fast ebbing away and the eternal frontiers within sight, Henri clung to his ideal republic, and we shall find him under the green trees at Sorèze, dreaming again the dream of his ardent youth, and building up with his beloved master, Lacordaire, "a new form of government, which shall constitute an alliance between Christianity and liberty, where men shall love God without hating one another." It was to this alliance of God and liberty alone that he looked for the regeneration of France. While that old bugbear of Europe, the Eastern problem, was being solved with cannon on the shores of the Black Sea, and the eyes of the West were watching for the eternal signs of conquest or defeat, Henri was steadily awaiting the one result whose consequences would endure, and whose victory would outlive the din of battle and the triumph of despotism. "A day will come," he writes to Adolphe Perraud, "when we must speak out, for words will then be actions, and it will be a duty for us even more than for others, because we have received from God two treasures seldom united in the same breast—the love of Jesus Christ and the love of liberty."

Bewailing the decay of these generous aspirations in the nation, he says to a friend on his return from the South : "I could not have conceived such a change in the public mind in so short a time ; the sleep of indifference has paralyzed everything, and people speak of liberty as a thing that has been sold ! After all, it is folly to think of founding a democracy when there is no longer a people. . . ."

But instead of dwelling in morbid despair on the political mistakes of France, he turned his eyes to more consoling subjects, and found consolation in the beauty of souls, the triumph of virtue, and the splendour of genius ; above all, in his love for God. His health, though improved by the winter in the South, was not much to be trusted, as he playfully tells us in describing a concert given for the benefit of a night-school which he had founded, and where he played the part of *cavaliere servente* to one of the lady collectors.

"There were about fifteen hundred persons present, and it was dreadfully hot. I might have passed on the duty to some one else, but the desire to play the dandy, etc., prevailed; so I gallantly took the lady by the hand, and made my *quête;* dress-coat, pumps, light gloves, etc. The result was that next day the dandy was in bed, with a cotton night-cap pulled over his ears, his nose swollen, and his throat on fire. . . . *Vanitas, vanitatum !"*

The friend to whom he makes this abject confession was himself in very bad health, and Henri was full of anxiety about him. "You have a cough, and you are not sure of going to the Eaux Bonnes. You must go, dear M. l'Abbé—you simply must. My little savings are at your disposal with all my heart; I have some time still to increase them, and by the end of August they may amount to a hundred francs. You have called me your friend so often, that I expect you will behave *generously* to me on this occasion."

The little hoard so lovingly offered was not, however, enough to pay for the journey to Eaux Bonnes, and Henri was amazed and shocked to find that other friends did not run as eagerly as himself to offer their savings to the sick priest. He determined to apply to the minister for the extra three hundred francs that were necessary, and relates the adventure with characteristic *verve.*

" . . . I made *grande toilette* and hurried off to the
Administration des Cultes at the Minister of Justice's.
I won't tell you what a business it was to approach such
a big-wig. After two hours' hard labour I succeeded !
I held forth, I explained, I argued. All in vain. The
sum was too large, and, above all, I suspect, the patronage
too small. I grew red in the face ; I stood up ; I prayed
to my imperturbable listener. I don't know what I said,
for I was a trifle excited by his refusal . . .

" The great man stared at me, and then all of a sudden
he said, ' *Allons, Monsieur*. I have not the heart to
hold out against you any longer !' With that he rose,
conducted me to his secretary, and ordered him to draw
up an order at once for the sum in question. The secretary was for putting it off, but he said, 'No ; I wish
it done immediately, signed to-morrow by the minister,
and despatched forthwith. I hold to this being done.'
. . . I embrace you joyfully. It is so seldom we have
a chance of proving to our friends that we really love
them."

A scheme for resuscitating the ancient Congregation of
the Oratory had for some time been germinating in the
minds of a few fervent souls, and Henri Perreyve was one
of those on whom they based their hopes for its accomplishment. He himself entered into it with delight.

" We are going to undertake a great work," he says ;
"three or four bishops are in the plot, and the Abbé
Gratry is at the head of it. . . . It is a great work—it is

enormous, and we are so little and so weak! This is
what is capable of moving the mercy of God."

He relates, in a touching page of his "Souvenirs of
Frederick Ozanam," how he first opened his heart on the
subject to that gentle master. It was at Eaux Bonnes,
and Henri was just going to start on a trip to Spain.
" Before leaving, I went to dine with M. Ozanam. That
evening we were sitting over the fire together, conversing
intimately about different things. I thought the moment
had come for confiding to that noble heart the secret of
my religious vocation. I did it simply, easily, with joy,
and yet with a kind of shyness. . . . That night I learned
what M. Ozanam's heart was. There were tears of affection, of fatherly indulgence, of holy enthusiasm, in the
voice that answered me. Our wish to serve God in the
cultivation of science and literature, our scheme of re-
union with M. l'Abbé Gratry, and of a studious congregation to be called the 'Oratory,' all these hopes, these
dreams, which might turn out to be illusions, quickly
took a living form in that soul which believed so readily
in all that was beautiful. . . . He followed me with
words of encouragement that night; he strained me to
his heart, and we parted. I walked quickly home, inebriated with joy and hope and strength. I could not
go in. I wanted to take my happiness in solitude, far
from men. It was very late; but I could not resist the
longing, so I struck into a road that led to the heights.
I walked on, beside myself with joy, not looking before

me, but looking up to heaven. Suddenly, I arrested my step, and an unconscious impulse made me start back; I was on the edge of a precipice. One step more and I had fallen into the abyss. I was frightened, and gave up my nocturnal promenade."

Before crossing over the Pyrenees, Henri wrote to a cousin of his, announcing the visit of a lady whose acquaintance he wished her to make.

". . . I have spoken of you to her, and she is very anxious to make friends with you. She is kind and good, and gracious and simple, although enjoying enormous wealth and in the very first society, where she occupies with distinction a high position; but in spite of her aristocracy she is charming in every way. . . . She will present herself at your door on Wednesday, between one and two o'clock. She will most likely take her little son with her; he is about three years old, and a little angel of beauty. Tell him from me that I don't forget the sweet smiles he gave me during my visits here. You may talk of him to his mother, who *adores* him, and you will present my respectful homage to her. Now, good-bye. Don't let this visit alarm you, and make no preparations to receive her. I am quite sure you will be delighted to have made an acquaintance which may one day prove most valuable to you. . . ."

At the hour and on the day named, his cousin received a box containing a lovely statue of Our Lady of Betharram. The dream of the restoration of the Oratory was

destined, unlike Henri's ideal republic, to take in reality
that living form which it at once assumed in the breast
of Frederick Ozanam. The history of the early days
of its existence reads like a page from the records of the
first Christians, so full of mutual love and joy and
enthusiasm were the young brotherhood. They lived
in a small house, big enough to hold seven, and here,
under the guidance of a saintly and learned priest, the
days flew swiftly in study and meditation on divine
things. They were halcyon days to Henri Perreyve, for
he found here, joined with him in the bonds of a divine
fraternity, the friends he had loved best from his
childhood.

"I cannot sufficiently admire the councils of God!"
he exclaims; "He prepared us by friendship before confiding His work to us; we had the same heart before
being joined in the same priesthood. The will of God
has but to communicate itself to one, in order to burst
out in hearts that are all so deeply united."

The moment the fact of his vocation became known
amongst his general circle of friends, Henri had to
endure the trial which awaits most souls under the same
circumstances—the lamentations of the world over his
cruel lot. He could laugh so long as it was only the
world that followed him to the sanctuary with its stupid
pity, but it was hard to bear patiently the commiseration
of good Christians, who, instead of giving him joy, be-
wailed and expostulated with him on thus throwing away
his life.

"It passes my comprehension," he cries, "how people who believe in the grandeur of the priesthood can be in despair at seeing a young man receive the favour of it! Can you bear to be pitied, M. l'Abbé? For my part, *I have a horror of it!*"

Eight days after his entrance into the Oratory (Nov. 8, 1853), he writes to an old friend: "You are right, Stephen, in thinking that the new life on which I am entering will diminish nothing of the warm affection God has given me for you. I am renouncing fully and absolutely all the joys and ambitions which at our age allure the soul; but there is one that I still cling to— that of being loved. It is a great deal; but I seem to feel that this sacrifice is not required of me."

St. Theresa said of the devil, "Poor wretch! he does not love." Henri's idea of heaven was a place where every one loved. "It is Arnaud, I think, who says that we shall have all eternity to rest; this notion of heaven does not smile on me at all; the idea of rest is fatiguing and inadequate, but, if you were to say, 'We shall have all eternity to love,' ah, then I should agree with you!"

Nor was it only that purest and most sublime love which possessed his own soul that he could admire and sympathize with. Whatsoever was holy, whatsoever was pure, whatsoever was brave and of good report, found an echo in his heart. He writes from the Oratory to a friend about to embrace the marriage state: ". . . Ah, Stephen, do not laugh at love, I implore of you, like

those fools who are incapable of feeling it. Do not
laugh at love. There is no more sacred word amongst
men. Love is not pleasure, it is not selfish enjoyment,
nor passion. The aim and end of love is sacrifice. . . .
You should sacrifice yourself in marriage as the priest
sacrifices himself in the priesthood, with devotion, with
entire self-surrender; with joy, if you will, but with a
sober joy which is akin to resignation and accepts
sorrow beforehand."

How sincere was his own self-surrender to the Crucified
Spouse who had chosen him, is touchingly manifested in
a note which we find in his private memorandum about
this time : " I have scarcely put on the blessed livery of
Thy service, Lord, and I have already received a stone
for Thy sake. It was yesterday in the street. The
stone was aimed by a strong hand, for it made a rent
in the wall where I was passing. I cannot describe the
sensation of pride and gratitude that thrilled my soul.
O my Lord, to suffer for Thee ! I was not worthy of
it. I have done nothing yet to deserve the honour ! "

On the day that he entered the Oratory, Henri received
a letter from a poor man whom he had been in the habit
of visiting in the prison of Sainte Pélagie. This is his
answer : " No, I don't forget you. Your letter was the
first that greeted me in this solitude to which the voice
of God has conducted me. What you say to me, even
your praise, unmerited as it is, did me good, and was
very precious to me just that day, for I was a little

cowardly and frightened, and I wanted some one to give me a helping hand to cross the threshold of the life I was entering on. . . . See how well Providence arranges things ! You have so often said that you never could do anything for me, and already you have done me a great service. Be assured of one thing ; we all want each other, and no one but a fool can say, ' That man will never be of any use to me !' . . . Here I am a prisoner like yourself—my wings clipped; and if there is one thing I have loved all my life, it is liberty—in theory and in practice."

And, through several pages, he continues in this tone of delicate and tender grace, drawing a parallel between his own position and that of the poor victim of human justice, encouraging him to imitate in humility and fortitude the Prisoner of Love, who made Himself a slave that we might be made free. The letter closes with these words :—

". . . Don't weary of blessing God for your misfortunes ; and if there does not come a moment when, in the full acceptance of the cross, the springs of consolation are suddenly opened to you, and a heaven of interior joy expands your soul until you are forced to cry out, ' What is this, my God, that my tears are changed to smiles, and I feel actually happy !'—if this moment does not come, then I will confess that I do not know my God, and that I understand nothing of His promises."

This "interior joy of heaven" was already given to him, who so boldly announced it as the inevitable reward of the "cross accepted," and this possession enabled him to speak with the irresistible force of experience and conviction.

"I will confess anything you like, madame," he says to a lady whom he was trying to convert to the faith, "but there still remains the fact that *I am happy*. The certainty of being where God wishes me to be, places my soul on a solid foundation of peace and calm. There are, no doubt, memories tinged with sadness; but there are no regrets. . . . There is, moreover, an indescribable charm in certain moods of the soul when it has just enough of *tristesse* to taste the full value of divine consolation. So, I beg of you, don't pity me! That would be very unjust, and very ungrateful to God, who has done, and is doing so much for me."

He was never tired impressing upon the souls who drew near him that suffering was the road to all true consolation, that joy was to be reached only through the cross, and that they only who had learned this lesson could teach it to others.

"Let me remind you," he says to a broken-hearted mother, "that great grief, accepted as becomes a Christian, gives to the soul a kind of unction, very fit to console the sufferings of others. You believe in *les graces d'état*, dear lady? Well, the state of resigned sorrow has a special grace for communicating resignation.

He who has not suffered is nearly always incapable of consoling others. . . . . Use this grace which has cost you so dear, and seek the company of those who are in sorrow."

One who was so richly endowed with spiritual gifts as Henri Perreyve could not remain unnoticed by those whose mission it is to discover and employ them. He had been about a year at the Oratory, when he was invited by the Dominican Fathers, on the feast of St. Dominic, to a banquet at which the Archbishop of Paris presided. After paying a tribute to the various religious orders represented amongst the guests, Monseigneur Sibour fixed his eyes steadily on Henri, and said, in a very significant manner, that he built hopes on him for the future.

"That is one of my little ones!" said Père Pététot, Superior of the Oratory.

"Let him be," replied his Grace; "he will grow to be a big one." Then turning to the young man, who sat overpowered with confusion : " My child," he added, "preserve in your heart what I have been saying until the will of God shall be accomplished in you."

Writing to Père Lacordaire next day, Henri says : "I am still full of our beautiful fête of yesterday. . . . One ought to die after a beautiful Christian festival. It is like a glimpse of heaven that makes the wings of one's soul beat; then the vision vanishes, and the veil drops, and to these strong interior lights which our Lord grants to His friends, there succeeds the dim twilight in which small souls dwell. I am one of them. . . . Father, I should so like to know if I am not deceiving myself in the love I have for death? I find in the thought of it treasures of joy, and it seems to me that there is not a moment in my life in which, were the choice given me to live or die, I should not choose death. And yet I am so happy! . . ."

His holidays this year (1854) were passed with the Dominican Fathers in their beautiful Convent of Chalais, and the visit was like one of those Christian festivals which Henri loved. The monks welcomed him "with a great fire and a great meal," the two forms of perfect hospitality.

"Oh, my friend," he writes, "I am transported. There is in this nature, regenerated by the habitation of saints, such an indescribable influence of prayer, chastity, and peace. . . . Yesterday we climbed to the top of Dauphiné; we saw the Alps with their chain of glaciers and snows sparkling against the sky, and towering above them all, Mont Blanc surrounded by its peaks, like a monarch by his guards and knights. I bethought me that at that hour you were perhaps contemplating the horizon of the sea, and I wondered which of us had the finest spectacle. But I was wrong. The greatness of God is in the sea, and His grandeur in the mountains. The sound of the waves is like the sound of the wind among the pine trees; the roll of

the mountains is like the surging of the billows; they
echo the same voice, and invite to the same prayer:
Mirabiles elationes maris, mirabilis in altis Dominus."

The beauty of the visible world was to him a reflexion
of the invisible beauty of God which it shadows forth to
the pure of heart. "I know not why it is," he says, "that
in contemplating the beauty of the mountains with a
young Dominican monk, we were led to admire the
beauty of the Blessed Virgin. Perhaps there is something more than a mere chance and indirect relation
between them. If physical nature is made according to
the image of God, and on the plans of the Eternal Word,
the human soul is still more truly His likeness, His
mirror; and of all souls that of the Blessed Virgin is
the most perfect likeness to the Divine soul. It is not,
therefore, strange that the incomplete beauty of nature
should remind us of the beauty of the most perfect of
creatures, and lead us to the contemplation of God, the
term of all beauty."

The desire of communicating to souls this knowledge
of their own beauty, and thus hastening on the coming
of God's reign, possessed his heart with ever-increasing
ardour.

"What a mission is ours, Adolphe!" he cries. "I
say it in trembling, in unutterable happiness—we are
a few chosen from among so many, and we have received
from God the *Divine secret.* The more I see of souls,
the more convinced I am that these grand ideas of social

and political progress by the rigorous application of the
evangelical doctrines are rare, and rarely granted. It
is astounding how little they have penetrated the hard,
dry soil of egotism ! . . . Yet they alone can save
France, they alone can save Christian civilization."

Henri returned from his visit to the Chalais refreshed
in body, and stimulated to new ardour in the pursuit
of his ideal. He resumed his work with great zest, but
it was very soon brusquely interrupted. He was seized
one morning in the street with a violent congestion of
the lungs ; he had burst a blood-vessel, and his life was
once more in jeopardy. Skilful care and complete rest
restored him for the time, but he knew that recovery
was doubtful, and likely, at best, to be only partial.

"The moment I felt myself stricken," he writes to
Père Lacordaire in the first days of convalescence, "the
idea of a broken, useless life presented itself to me ;
but the very danger of my position brought a sort of
consolation with it. I thought I was going to die, I
waited for death, I hoped for it, I asked for it. It so
happened I had been meditating on death lately a good
deal; I had looked over my will, and made a good
retreat, during which I felt for the first time, perhaps,
the joy of an unbounded abandonment to the will of
God, and the hope of a life sacrificed for the service
of truth and justice. In fact, I felt ready to go, and
I was waiting for death, full of consolation and spiritual
joy. But God would not have me. He flung me back

into the world, and now I have got to live in it with
the dread before me of a future without strength, disarmed,
useless. . . . Father, can you imagine what such a life
must be for a soul that hoped to work and to fight? A
life of ease and cowardice, fictitiously supported, of no
use to any one or anything. This prospect has given
me more pain than all the rest. I try to turn away from
it, but in vain; it is an *idée fixe* that devours me."

The allied armies were suffering gloriously in the
East, and Henri's heart swelled with grief at not being
able to go and solace his countrymen. "Instead of
taking care of myself and lying quiet, if I were a
priest now," he cries, "I would beg leave to go out
as chaplain to the Crimea. What is to become of me
this winter? And my theology only just begun! . . .
Pray for me. I know I must accept the will of God;
but can I accept as such a life contrary to all He wills
me to do? If He means me to be in His service, can
He mean me to be an invalid, useless, sterile in
works? . . . I cannot, I *ought* not to believe this.
I will do what God wishes me to do, or I will die. Is
it not so, Father?"

If the voice of the natural will is too clearly heard in
this passionate appeal, it will serve to show later on how
perfectly the triumph of the Divine will had been accomplished in a soul, as yet not entirely purified from self,
but whose whole energies were bent upon the noble
conquest. Henri regained sufficient strength to resume

a certain amount of work, and the following letter reveals something of the spirit in which it was performed, and the rewards it brought him.

"I had a nice day yesterday. . . . I had the happiness of coming in contact with two beautiful souls. The first was the soul of a child, a little soul of twelve years old. You never saw anything so beautiful! Imagine the most sparkling diamond, the most limpid crystal, and you will hardly have even the symbol of this soul. I went to see the child in a convent where she is being brought up. God withdrew her, almost by a miracle, from the most dangerous surroundings, and placed her in this atmosphere of light and peace. The little creature feels His hand upon her soul. Her heart is a perpetual thanksgiving. She talks already of the religious life.* I said to her, 'Marie, you must not think of that yet awhile; you are only a child now;' but I said interiorly to God, 'Take her Lord. She is worthy of You!' Another soul—a friend of my childhood, a poor young fellow of my own age, brilliant, rich, launched in the world, and *lost*, unless God saves him. He has faith, but . . . well, he has a beautiful soul for all that. •But·what a different kind of beauty from the first! It is beautiful as a ruin; beautiful because it suffers. . . . I cannot tell you the compassion I feel for that soul. Nothing can be more beautiful, cast down and broken as it is. . . . This has taught me many things, and how our Lord could give His blood for such an object of love."

No wonder that one so keenly alive to the beauty of souls should have suffered in no small degree from seeing these likenesses of God debased and blurred, even when not utterly broken, by the unhealthy influences of our artificial life.

"The life of souls here below is a sad and curious spectacle," he says. "Take a bird, tie its wings so that it cannot fly, gag its throat so that it cannot sing, put a bandage round its eyes so that it cannot see ; then shut it up in a narrow cage in company with an immense number of other poor birds arranged in the same fashion ; then watch the awkward movements, the discomfort, the clumsy, blundering ways, the misery of this crowd of prisoners, without sight, or voice, or power of flying, and I think you will have a very fair representation of the life of souls in human society."

A feeling that he was himself maimed and cramped in his power of working for these souls whom he loved so dearly, awoke in his heart an intense desire to, at least, suffer something for them. Prompted by this feeling, in a moment of extraordinary fervour he asked God to send him a humiliation. The prayer was answered almost immediately. Let him relate the incident himself.

" A circumstance in which I had acted rather giddily, out of kindness and to oblige another, brought me in contact with a personage whom I will not name, but who was the offended party. This man treated me as a wretch ; he overpowered me with the most unjust reproaches, and imposed silence on me when I tried to answer. I, naturally so quick and hasty, felt crushed by his violence, and incapable of defending myself. The next day I knew what a wound was. I had a thirst, a fever for reparation that was like a physical suffering. I had utterly forgotten my prayer and my promises, and I demanded the reparation. It was no sooner done than I *remembered !* It was rather late. I did what I could, and I forgave. But the whole thing has left in me a sort of interior soreness which is dreadful. . . . All this is cowardly. I am not a man. Forgive me. I hope to become one."

He was blessed with a natural gaiety, which added a great charm to his spiritual and intellectual gifts ; he prized it himself, even in the spiritual order, and was on the watch to guard against the depression which bodily suffering is so apt to engender. He combated in himself and others a tendency to melancholy, as the result of embittered self-love unworthy of a Christian.

" What, do I hear of your being constantly in tears ? " he writes to a relative. "I have never read anywhere that the Blessed Virgin had a *maladie noire* (blue devils), and yet the Blessed Virgin had terrible trials. And, for that matter, is not everybody's malady a black malady ? Do you imagine mine is rose-coloured ? When I see myself incapable of doing anything, whilst all my friends are working away, and that I am ' becoming a dunce,' as my old Bonne says, do you suppose this is not black to me? But instead of crying over it, I try to laugh; and when one has said resolutely, 'No, I won't be cast down; God does not try us above our strength; there are thousands in Paris more to be pitied than I am,' . . . and such-like thoughts, courage returns, and we find ourselves on our feet."

Speaking of himself in a moment of great physical suffering and prolonged inaction, he says: "It would grieve me if I were to grow sad; people don't like sad priests. I hope to get back my gaiety."

And so he did; or rather he never lost it; the sadness which he fought against so unselfishly was never more than a passing cloud, which lent a fresh charm to the brightness that soon returned. He got through the winter without any serious accident, but the warm weather was the signal for his departure again to Eaux Bonnes. After the usual course of waters, he went for a time to Biarritz (August 7, 1855).

"I have been visiting a community of nuns extraordinarily edifying—holy women, who devote their lives to directing poor penitent girls. These latter are admirable; they dig the earth; they possess nothing, give themselves up to the most rigorous penance, and for their reward aspire to become *Bernardines*. And this is what a Bernardine is—a holy soul who lives on the sands of the sea-shore, like the early anchorites of the deserts of Africa. She eats black bread and drinks water; she *never speaks*, . . . mind, *never!* The Chartreux

speak once a week ; she, never. She dies after this long
martyrdom, in which she has regained more honour and
innocence than she has lost in her wanderings. The
last who died—they showed me the newly made grave
—expired saying, 'How joyful it is to die when one
loves God !' This is what I call a happy death. Will
ours be like it?"

The effect of the waters, though beneficial, was far
from being complete, and his friends, more uneasy than
they dared confess, proposed to make a great, general
novena for his recovery. The invalid heard of it, and
was grateful; but he had made long strides in the way
of the cross since that passionate appeal to be allowed
"to do what God meant him to do, or die."

"I don't ask for deliverance from this trial," he writes
to an anxious friend ; " I have seen too clearly how much
the road to truth is shortened by passing through suffering to recoil from being led that way. I have a horror
of it, a natural horror ; for there does not exist a being
less fit to suffer than I, nor one more easily frightened ;
more restive, more liable to exaggerate the evil ; more
accessible to anguish of soul ; but I offer even this want
of strength, this faint-heartedness, these childish fears,
this weariness of spirit, to Him who in the garden of
Olives began to tremble and to be sorrowful even unto
death."

Before returning to Paris, Henri paid a visit to Sorèze.
"A delicious week in the constant society of Père

Lacordaire, who spoiled me more than ever," he says; and he goes on to relate an episode of the visit which affected him deeply. "One of my great delights here has been hearing the Father read his notice on M. Ozanam. . . . Fancy, he quotes two whole pages of the little *mémoires* * I sent him six months ago! I was quietly listening to the reading when suddenly I recognized the thoughts, then the author. . . . I grew scarlet, and the drops stood on my forehead. I protested—honestly—but to no purpose. So I shall be printed in the works of Père Lacordaire! It is enough to confound me and make me sink into the earth. . . . Don't tell this to anybody. . . ."

The improvement which he brought back from Eaux Bonnes did not seem to warrant his spending the winter in Paris. The doctors decided that he must return to Italy. His hopes of receiving the subdiaconate at Christmas in the venerable old church of St. Sulpice, where he had made his First Communion, were thus disappointed. Henri bowed his head unmurmuringly, but the pang was none the less bitter.

On the 3rd of November, he writes from Nice: ". . . On All Saints' morning, after Communion, I renewed the pledges to which, when taking the habit two years ago, we committed ourselves. I was very happy,

---

* These two pages, the most tenderly poetic, perhaps, of any that H. Perreyve has left us, are quoted in full by the present writer in the Life of Ozanam.

D

full of consolation and strength, and I am still walking
in the light of the graces given me in that Communion.
The rest of the day I spent at the great military hospital
at Marseilles, where our wounded soldiers from the East
daily disembark. It was one of the deepest impressions
of my life. I felt proud and happy, amazed and humbled,
by the confidence which these brave fellows showed me ;
many amongst them were dying, some were in their
agony. If I had been a priest I might have confessed
over thirty of them. Their wounds are dreadful, and
their accounts of the winter and of the taking of Sebas-
topol are awful. We have no idea of what they have
suffered. You can't think how sad it is to hear these
tales of glory and battle on the lips of poor young fellows
who for three months and more have been lying on a
bed of pain, weakened by fever, with wounds that have
festered in the long and painful journey, and who, after
these great labours, have before them nothing but a
broken and useless career. . . . I wish I could give you
an idea of the really *holy* look with which many of them
said to me, ' I have done my duty, M. l'Abbé ; may the
will of God be done ! ' This word duty is in every
mouth. I was much struck by it, and it has filled me
with an immense hope for France."

Such foretastes of those divine consolations which await
the priest in his ministry only made Henri hunger the
more for the day when his life should be filled with
them ; but he was learning in the school of the Cross to

become more worthy of them. His life had a daily, nay,
hourly struggle between the too willing spirit and the
fainting flesh.

"I am not sure," he says, "if there is not a new
source of energy and vigour for thought in the constant
effort of the mind struggling against the hindrances of
disease. One works somewhat as one fights. So I am
satisfied with my condition until the next break-down,
and perhaps you will read some day an essay entitled,
La liberté de l'Eglise, which may be born of this struggle.
Ah ! the liberty of the Church. Let us love it, Eugène !
Let us two swear to love it, to love it always, to serve it
always."

One of the first consolations which awaited him in
Rome was receiving Holy Communion from the hands
of Pius IX. It was on the feast of St. Agnes. The
spectacle of the pomp with which the Church celebrates
the glory of the humble maiden martyred seventeen
centuries ago, woke deep emotions in Henri's soul.

". . . Two little white lambs, ornamented with flowers
and streamers, are blessed by the Pope, and their wool
is used for weaving the palliums. How true it is that
the most beautiful vestment of the church is woven by
pure hearts, by the innocence of her virgins, and the
chastity of her priests !"

A few days later, he "had the privilege of being presented to" Cardinal (then Dr.) Newman, by Father
Ambrose St. John. "Father Newman is a man of infinite

sweetness and kindness, with none of the English stiffness, and full of the loftiest ideas concerning the religious future of England. He gave me precious details as to what one may hope for in that noble country, so naturally pious and earnest. F. Newman said to me, 'We only want priests.' Alas ! . . . Our conversation was of the funniest ; he understands French, but answers in Italian ; I consequently spoke to him in French ; then I had to speak Italian to Father St. John, who does not speak French ; finally, they spoke English to one another. Ideas made their way through this Babel, and I don't think one went astray."

Another distinguished personage whose acquaintance Henri made in Rome was Cardinal Villecourt, who became his patron and opened every door to him.

" . . . I reminded him, as you told me," he writes to his father, "of the old servant who used to say at Fourvières, 'Little Villecourt will be a priest.' He laughed heartily, and bade me remember him to you. He makes great fun of me in his gentle way, and says, 'Do you suppose that, because I am a Cardinal and sixty-eight years old, I have not the right to laugh ?' He leads the life of a hermit in Rome, and cannot accustom himself to the grand ways of the purple. When he was named Cardinal, he never slept for eight days ; but, as the intention of the Pope was still a secret, he could not confide his trouble to any one. His old servant, John, used to say to him, 'Monseigneur has some trouble that he won't tell me.' And he would reply, 'What will you, my poor John? such an unlikely thing has befallen us !' 'If it is a case of going to the ends of the earth, why can you not tell me? you know well that I will follow you.' At last the day came, and the good Bishop said to John, 'My poor John, I am a Cardinal !' John did not know whether to laugh or cry; but since he has seen *laquais* in the anteroom, and become himself the majordomo of a large establishment, they say he makes the best of being a Cardinal. Is there not something very touching and *mœurs d'autrefois* about it all? . . '. Good-bye, dear father; your son embraces you, and his mother, and his good old Rose,* who is his *vieux Jean*, and prays God to bless you."

The question of his being admitted to orders had been discussed since his arrival in Rome, and after a good deal of hesitation, his health being the only obstacle, it was decided that he should be ordained on Trinity Sunday.

His joy on receiving this sentence flows from his heart with an eloquence that gives some idea of its intensity: "Oh, what a heart I ought to have ! A new heart ! My friend, as you love Jesus Christ, ask Him to change my heart for *that day*. I cannot bear the thought of offering Him on that beloved day of our spiritual nuptials a heart so poor in virtue, so small, so full of self ! Ask for me that which I have not. Commend

* An old servant who had brought him up.

me to the prayers of holy souls. I tell you I am unworthy of this unspeakable honour. In pity for me, ask
of God to build Himself the temple in which He is to
dwell, and to purify His own tabernacle." And, a few
days later to another friend: " . . . Eugène, pray for
me. . . . Let our joy be full. . . . Let us lift up our
hearts ; let us look at the beauty of the divine plan. It
is all too beautiful ! Who has made the advances in this
mystery of love wherein Jesus and we are but one soul ?
Who has never grown weary of loving with infinite
delicacy, and, alas ! with infinite patience ! Who but
Jesus, our Master, our Lord ! . . . We are not worth
the trouble of saying that we are worth nothing. Let us
only speak of Jesus. . . . Friend, I embrace thee at His
feet. God forbid we should be priests, you and I, if it
were not to love Jesus unto death ! Amen."

That day, which was waited for with such transports
of joy, came at last. On the Feast of the Holy Trinity,
Henri Perreyve was ordained subdeacon at the Church
of St. John of Lateran.

"What shall I say to thee, my mother?" he writes
home the next day. . . . "It is all over; or rather, it is
begun. The blessed ceremony was more imposing, more
full of grace and emotion than I had hoped. I prostrated
myself with a willing heart on the pavement of the *Mother
of Churches,* to promise to God that immortal fidelity which
your prayers will enable me to keep. The ordination
was performed by the Cardinal Patrizi, whom you will

see one of these days in Paris for the imperial christen-
ing. . . . After this grand morning, we received our kind
neighbours, who made our feast theirs. Need I say how
much I missed thee, mother dear, and my father and my
old Rose! My sister was very happy, and gave me some
compensation for your absence. . . . Sunday I saw the
Holy Father, and presented him with a copy of the
unpublished part of my work on the Immaculate Con-
ception. The binding was splendid, at any rate, and
the Holy Father promised me to have the inside examined. . . . A great many people came to my ordination. Monsieur Ampère remained the whole time, and
coming out he pressed my hands with tears in his eyes.
What a beautiful soul! He brought a young French
painter with him, who seemed deeply impressed by the
ceremony."

About a month later the young deacon made his usual
pilgrimage to Eaux Bonnes, stopping at Sorèze on his
way thither, for the fête of Père Lacordaire. He was
called upon suddenly to make a speech at the dinner-
table before two hundred and fifty persons, and was
surprised to find that his voice had regained something
of its former power and sonority. "I was greatly
moved," he writes to his mother, "which was a reason
for moving others; but what encourages me is that this
emotion, instead of crushing, sustained and carried me
with it. I tell you this in all filial simplicity. Père
Lacordaire said to me afterwards, in *tête-à-tête*, ' My dear

friend, you will be a speaker.' But for this one must have lungs, and it is the want of them that brings me again to Eaux Bonnes."

During his stay at the waters, he met M. Cousin, and he informs Père Gratry of his glad surprise in discovering how near that noble mind had come to catholic ideas. " Let us pray for these souls," he says, "and above all let us not make the doors of the Church bristle with razors and pikestaffs, and pitchforks, and bundles of thorns."

The waters proved so beneficial this season that on his return to Paris Henri writes to Père Lacordaire : " I feel wonderfully better this year, and the doctors protest that they believe in my cure." But notwithstanding this protest, they insisted on his returning for the winter to Rome, where his stay was to be more of an exile this year, as his sister did not accompany him.

" . . . Dear one," he writes to her, " I cannot understand why I should not set off to the *Via della Vita* in half an hour from this, and sit warming myself with you over the fire. Yesterday evening, I could not resist going to look up at the house ; there was light in the windows and I could fancy . . . but all that is swept away with the shadows of the past. . . . Life has assumed a graver aspect for me ; I am tasting the life of the poor lonely student in Paris. It is well. One ought to learn what these ordeals are. Up to the present, I should not have known how to confess those poor young fellows who are ill at ease in a hotel by themselves; to-morrow, I should know better how to go about it. One only knows really the various conditions of the soul by experiencing them one's self."

But he found delights in his solitary life which soon made it dear to him. "I have a little apartment rather far from all my acquaintances," he writes to a friend in Paris. "I fly from visits as much as I can, for I love my solitude. I suffer now and then, when souvenirs crowd in on me; but I have a horror of people who want to divert my mind (*me distraire*). Divert it from what? Good heavens! From that ardent, living, interior life with God, where I dwell with the souls I love. Ah, how infinitely I prefer, to all the diversions of the world, the hours, mayhap a little shaded with regret, which I pass in this dear company."

On the feast of St. Gregory he tells Père Gratry—"I have just served the venerable Doctor Manning's Mass in the fine church of the great Saint who rests under the shadow of the Coliseum. . . . The famous Doctor Palmer had come to fetch us, and went to Communion with us. His is one of those souls conquered by the irresistible violence of the Lamb, and who have broken all their ties rather than let go the hand of Jesus Christ. I can't tell you what I feel in seeing these English converts in the sanctuaries of Rome; they bear on their brow the glory of the great sacrifices they have made, and of a conscience satisfied at every cost—exiled, and yet come back to their true country, having lost all, and yet found all. . . .'

He was hard at work meantime, and engaged, amidst his studies, on a treatise entitled, "Entretiens sur l'Eglise Catholique," which appeared on his return to Paris. He made a retreat before leaving Rome, and some of his meditations during those days of silence with God have been preserved to us by Père Gratry in his notice of Henri Perreyve.

On coming out of this interval of solitude he announces to a friend that his ordination as deacon is fixed for the end of May, on his return to Paris.

"I was very happy in my retreat, Charles. . . . Ah! what a friend we have in Jesus Christ! What indulgence! What a drawing near of His Heart to ours at the foot of the Altar! . . . I shall embrace you on the eve of the day when we two shall prostrate ourselves together at the feet of our Lord to receive the holy order of deacon. We will join our prayers, our graces, our meditations; we will share everything. . . . I embrace you at the feet of Jesus."

His birthday came round before he left Rome.

"I am six and twenty to-day! It is dreadful! And with that I have discovered that I know nothing, and that I have done nothing! . . . Alas! how do I burn with impatience to do something for souls in the name of Jesus Christ! You are in the secret of this interior fire, which so wore me out at Eaux Bonnes, and which follows

me everywhere. Where are the souls I am to teach and
to love? Where are the ears of that sheaf which the
priest gleans amidst tears and anguish? Where are my
children? I see no sign of their coming yet. You talk
of my writings. . . . It is a hundred times better worth
while to confess a rag-and-bone man than to write a
clever article in a fashionable magazine; but where is
my rag-and-bone man? It is him I am on the look-
out for!"

His return to Paris, and impending ordination, seemed
to bring him nearer to this object of his search, but the
cross of the divine will once more placed itself between
him and that other cross, which he so thirsted to embrace.
On the second day of his retreat at St. Sulpice, preparatory to his ordination, he was seized with congestion
of the lungs and a cough that racked him day and night.
He kept up by sheer stress of will till the Saturday, when,
during the solemn prostration, he drew his handkerchief
from his mouth soaked in blood.

"That day so longed for," he says, relating the incident
to a friend when all was over, "that day of special graces
of the Lord, was also a day of great fatigue. The
ceremony was barely over when I had just time to get
home, and the doctor was sent for. They bled me,
and since then I have been from one remedy to another.
I am now better; but here is another trial, a fresh proof
of my uselessness, a new humiliation for my soul. . . .
But God sees that I am not pure enough, since He does

not accept me. . . . Ah! how true it is what you
say, Eugène, that we should give our whole heart to
Him who always gives more love than He receives.
How is it that we do not understand that His incom-
parable love is the one thing necessary! . . . What
madness it is to hold in our hands the supreme Beauty,
the supreme Good, Love without end, and yet . . . to
go on suffering and complaining, and never make an
end of it!"

Henri's complaint was not that of those who murmur
and are destroyed. Joy was the strong cry of his soul,
despite the blow which love had again dealt at him.

"Well, at last I am a deacon!" he says to Père
Gratry, "and you will see if, by dint of good will, I
don't arrive, little by little, at the priesthood. *Introibo
ad altare Dei!* I hope to bring to it a heart inebriated
with the love of God and souls!" "I asked our Lord
to take my *whole* heart in this ordination," he says;
"and I hope He did. The Abbé B——, a beautiful
soul, with gifts and lights of inconceivable richness,
preached the sermon. What a living soul! What a
heart! What rays of light! It produced on me the
effect of a warm, glowing atmosphere. Eugène, *let us
love.* If we mean ever to speak of souls to men, *let
us love.* . . ."

The first breath of winter was the signal for his departure to the South. He rested a little while at Sorèze,
and came in while there for the great fête of the school

on St. Cecilia's day. All the notabilities of the town
were present, and Henri was called on for a speech
He felt more sure of himself on this occasion than he
had done the preceding year. "I don't know how it
was that I felt sufficiently master of myself to taste
even the pleasure of the thing," he says to his friend,
Charles Perraud. "Verily, I can understand that it
must be an immense delight, above all when one speaks
for the salvation of souls, for God. But what perils
lurk in the exercise of this gift! How deeply it pene-
trates the heart, agitating us, thrilling us with a sense
of power, even when it has done nothing, or next to
nothing. . . . What must it be in the case of successful
effort, of an oratorical triumph! Ah, let us prepare
our souls to receive these shocks without weakness,
without betraying the cause of our Master, to whom
alone and always praise and honour are due."

He was now beginning to count the days till the dawn
of that day to which he had aspired unceasingly since
his First Communion. His health was still very pre-
carious, and he was spitting blood again ; but the more
the body flagged, the more the spirit burned. "The
one thing serious amidst all this," he says, exultingly,
"is that in six months I am going to be a priest! Alas!
how I ought to shake with fear before this awful prerogative, so overpowering to my weak nature. . . . In
deed and in truth I blush as I write these lines, so
conscious am I of my unworthiness to guide souls for

the glory of Jesus Christ. . . . You will pray for me, will you not? and get all the holy souls you can to pray for me."

His friend Charles Perraud was ordained during his absence, and Henri thus greets the young priest on the morning of his divine espousals :—

" . . . May the Lord be with thee, dear brother ! With thee this morning at the altar of thy first Mass, to accept thy nuptial vows, to answer them with that reciprocity of love which passes all love ! . . . With thee to-morrow to make thee feel that the joy of God, unlike the joys of this world, is perpetual, and to be tasted for ever, while never satiating ! With thee, when, after these sacred inebriations, thou wilt feel what it is to be a priest for men, and to descend from Thabor to go to those who suffer, to those who are ignorant, to those who hunger and thirst after light and life ! With thee in thy sorrows, to console thee ! With thee in thy joys, to sanctify them ! With thee, my Charles, if thou art to be left alone in life, with only the arm of the Divine Friend to lean on ! With thee in thy young priesthood ! With thee, grown old in the service of God and man ! . . . May the Lord be with thee ! Charles, bless me. I embrace thee on the heart of the beloved Divine Master."

The heart which uttered this sweet canticle of love had now come too near that of "the Divine beloved Master" to have a wish, however holy, that was not

in perfect conformity to His will. Henri had reached
that point where the soul, called upon to make the
sacrifice of its sacrifice, answers with unhesitating fidelity,
"Behold the servant of the Lord!"

"Listen to me, my Charles," he writes to the newly
anointed priest a few days later; "listen to me. This
morning, amidst those burning desires for the priesthood
which have possessed me lately, a feeling stronger than
all this seemed to pervade my soul. I felt that I was
ready to sacrifice even *that joy of joys, that sole aim of
my whole life* (cette unique raison de toute ma vie) to
the will of God, and I accepted to die to-morrow without having gone up to the Altar, notwithstanding that
this death would be to me a sacrifice of a thousand lives,
a sorrow of a thousand deaths."

The God whom Henri had come to love with this
entire generosity was not likely to rob His servant of
"that joy of joys." In spite of his sufferings, his
strength seemed renovated so as to enable him to
compass the work demanded by the final examinations.

"I rise at a quarter to six," he writes from Hyères
to his father, "and serve Père Gratry's Mass in the
neighbouring chapel at half-past six; we come in and
work from half-past seven till half-past eleven. This
is a good pull. After breakfast, promenade from half-
past twelve till three; from three to six work again;
at six we meet to discuss some subject of religion or

controversy; then comes supper, *soirée* till half-past eight, breviary at nine, and then the curfew bell."

A severe relapse interrupted the even tenor of this programme, but nothing could disturb the peace of perfect conformity which the sufferer's soul had attained. ". . . I was in bed, ill, far from my own people, tended by a kind Sister of Charity, in that state of union with Jesus on the Cross which tempers the soul so vigorously when one accepts it with faith and love. I made the sacrifice for both of us; and from that moment, every time I kiss my crucifix I place you with myself in the Heart of the Divine Master. There is nothing, *nothing* for us now in this world but complete and boundless abandonment into the arms of Jesus Christ. . . . We are His. Let us love His rights, and defend them against the miserable faint-heartedness of our own will. . . . No more cowardice— no more weakness. Whatever God wills !"

Père de Ravignan's death, which occurred at this time (on the 4th March, 1858), drew a tribute of tender regret and reverence from the kindred soul of Henri: ". . . What a death !" he cries; "if we can call death a sigh somewhat fainter, which marks the entrance of a saint into his triumph. What words on that death-bed round which shone the halo of a whole life of sacrifice ! He kept repeating with the ardour of a wounded soldier, ' *Fight, fight, fight the battles of the Lord !* ' And when in the middle of the night the friend who was watching by him, Père de Ponlevoy, seeing by certain signs that

death was at hand, said to him, 'Come, brother, you are
going to die !' the holy religious, with that austere smile
that you know so well, said, 'Ah ! at last, *merci !*' And
we call this dying? And we fear death? . . ."

The departure of Père Gratry was a trial to Henri,
not merely in the loss of his companionship, but because
it deprived him of daily mass. He was now only able
to assist at the holy sacrifice three times a week, and
then in the face of a biting cold wind. Nevertheless,
he managed to continue his theological studies without
a break; although his health "threatens ruin from day
to day, from one cause or another."

"What I shall be able to do in the diocese with this
fine instrument I know not," he says, laughingly ; "I am
in a state of uncertainty, and I must remain in it until our
Lord passes this way and says to me, 'Arise and come !'
Meanwhile, I am learning not to despise small efforts and
small results, as probably my life is destined to be spent
in such. I have often said that nothing would give me
more real joy than to teach the catechism to children,
and should the day come when I am called on to renounce
all the lofty ambitions of my boyhood, I will readily console myself in these lowly tasks."

The infirm state of health which threatened to shut
him out from the larger action of the ministry did not
prevent him from exercising a very active and salutary
kind of priesthood around him. His holiness made him
an object of general veneration, and his counsel and

presence were sought for by numbers, especially amongst those higher classes against whom he entertained strong prejudices. Like most prejudices, they were the result of ignorance. He had not as yet come in contact with the society which he judged so severely; but he was quick in acknowledging his error as soon as he recognized it.

". . . Just fancy me launched in spite of myself amongst the very highest aristocracy! I was requested to go to the Duke and Duchess de —— to give religious instruction to a little child of theirs. Other acquaintances grew out of this one, and now it is high time I left this place, for I am in the midst of dukes, marquises, and viscounts. These people are all good, at least those of them that I see. Their faults are different from the faults • of our class; but they have qualities that I did not know of. Men misjudge each other half the time for want of knowing each other, and this is what happened to me with regard to the aristocracy. I have found amongst them women who are modest, pious, and charitable, and I find much less haughtiness than I expected. The malady of these people is idleness. The young men are all in danger of having their youth blighted by pleasure and the abuse of fortune. For this reason many families are now endeavouring to give them a career, and thus render them more useful to themselves and their country. A wise and excellent tendency. So much for the result of my aristocratic observations."

But while ready to make the full *amende honorable* to the class which he had judged in ignorance, Henri's sympathies remained true to the lowly ones whom his Master loved. Writing to a soul whom he was helping to pass through a great sorrow, he says : " I am glad to find that you are not confining yourself to a school for poor children; God has endowed you with gifts which will enable you to do for young girls of distinction what many others are incapable of doing ; but for the benefit as well as the consolation of your soul, I advise you to devote yourself chiefly to the care of the poorer classes. What we do for well-bred, intelligent children is a source of pleasure ; we reap the fruits of it easily, and often it becomes a source of vanity ; whereas, what we do for the poor is generally devoid of all pleasure, and has no earthly reward ; it is much easier to do it purely for the love of Jesus Christ, and therefore to derive great merit from it. At least, this is what I have always felt when I have been charged with the instruction of the children of the rich and of the poor."

The month of May arrived, and Henri was back in Paris, trying to realize the stupendous joy that was now fast advancing. The ordination was to take place on the 29th. Before entering on retreat, he writes to one friend : " Pray for me. *I am actually going to be a priest !* I can hardly believe it, the weight of my unworthiness seems so to draw me away from the grace. Yet God has so willed it ! Oh, abyss of mercy ! . . . Dear friend, if I have ever scandalized or pained, or disedified you, in the course of my life, I humbly ask your pardon. Oh, in days like these how one longs to have been always good, always pure! How the memory of faults weighs us down! We have nothing for it but to take refuge in the abyss of infinite mercy, and to recall those words of the Master: *Non vos me elegistis, sed ego elegi vos. . . .*"

To another friend he says: "I come to announce to you my priestly consecration. Let me repeat to your heart this astounding fact, which I scarcely believe in myself: *I am going to be a priest!* I tremble. Who would not tremble before such an honour! But I above all others, for I know my weakness, my unworthiness. . . . Pray for me. I have often told you, and now I repeat it to you with special joy: all this dates from my First Communion. That day Jesus proposed to me to follow Him, and I answered Him, 'Yes, beloved Lord, I am Thine for ever!' . . . Oh, abyss of divine mercy! Unfathomable depths of the eternal decrees! . . . Give thanks to God with me for having kept me faithful to the promises of my First Communion!"

An old family servant is not forgotten in the midst of his overflowing joy: "I wish you, my dear Micol, and your family to share in this blessed fête of my first Mass. I send you, with my affectionate remembrances, a post-office order for ten francs. You will buy something for the children or for the *ménage*, and you will say, 'This is a souvenir of the Abbé Henri's first Mass.'

I regret very much that I can't make it more, but the fact is, this is the end of my purse, and there remains to me at this moment thirty-six sous. Adieu, pray for me. Above all, I ask for the prayers of your children. It is actually true that on next Saturday I shall be a priest, and that on Sunday I shall celebrate Mass! Ah! if you knew how unworthy I am of this excess of honour! . . ."

After eight days' of solitary communion with God, the morning of this awful and magnificent grace dawned. On the 29th May, 1858, in the church of St Sulpice, Henri Perreyve was ordained a priest. The next day he went up to the altar.

"My first Mass was beautiful," he says; "Père Lacordaire was faithful to the rendez-vous. He came from Sorèze to assist me at the altar and to protect me before God by his great sacerdotal virtues. . . . Now I belong solely and absolutely to God, and I wait to know from Him in what way He means to make use of me. I have but one desire in my soul—to be a good priest, chaste and humble, to serve our beloved Master as He wills: in obscurity, before the world, in active ministry, in study, with my pen, or with my tongue. *A son bon plaisir!* The obstacle to everything still is my health. I assure you it is only a vigorous act of blind faith that enables me to think of remaining here next winter and undertaking a fixed service."

He set out to the Eaux Bonnes in July, by way of

bracing himself for the winter campaign. On his way to the Pyrenees he stayed a week at Sorèze, where a great but startling grace·awaited him.

He writes in his private memorandum : "Yesterday, one of the most beautiful days of my life, I performed the first act of my ministry. I confessed a soul, a great soul. This soul, the first that humbled itself at my feet, and laid its secrets in my breast, is the same that raised me up in the first days of my youth, Père Lacordaire. He wanted to do it for several days : he said to me, ' Henri, you must hear my confession.' I hesitated, I felt myself so little ! I prayed God to enlighten me, and I came to see that it was a great design, worthy of two souls who loved each other in God. So yesterday I went to him and said, ' I am ready.' He laid bare his whole life to me from the age of six to his conversion, and from his conversion up to the present day. Lord, what dost Thou will? For it is not like Thee to reveal these great things to a soul from whom Thou willest nothing. . . . May these souvenirs, so beautiful in themselves, fertilized by Thy grace, make of my life one long oblation, one sacrifice ! "

His next sacramental function was performed in the service of a soul very different, but also dear, that of an aged relative who was much attached to him.

" . . . I must tell you," he writes from Eaux Bonnes, "that in the midst of my present utter vacuity God has granted me a great grace. I was enabled to reconcile to God on his death-bed one of my uncles who had given up all practise of religion since his childhood. They ran to fetch me when he was dying; the poor man would have nobody but me, and I had to do every- thing. Certainly it is an honour a hundred thousand- fold too great for me that our Lord should make use of me to bring back one soul to Him. But these are baits which excite one's hunger for the apostolate, instead of appeasing it. Pray for me. I don't forget that it is through prayers, through the masses that were said for me, that I obtained the grace to live, against all appear- ances, until I became a priest. I firmly believe that God, by a positive and extraordinary miracle, may communi- cate to a natural remedy, such as the waters, a special efficacy for one person, and bless the remedy so as to give it a sovereign power. Pray, that if the little strength I may regain is to serve to the glory of God it may be given to me. If not, I ask for nothing but peace of mind and a speedy end."

The latter prayer seemed the one that was to be granted. On his return to Paris, the Abbé Perreyve writes, after a serious relapse : "I am a little better, but the improvement is almost imperceptible, and the effects of the illness will last a long time. God's will be done. I may own to you that I consider this illness one of the greatest graces I have received for a long time, and I wanted it badly. It has made a great impression on me, and has shown me by the light of the eternal frontiers

what the priesthood really is, and what God has a right
to expect of a priest."

The death of his old nurse, "ma vieille Rose,"
occurred soon after, and the regrets that it draws forth
from the young priest reveal the tenderness of his
human affections, and present a charming picture of
what is fast becoming an extinct type in the domestic
relations of these days of progress.

" . . . I have sad news for you. Our dear old Rose
died on Monday, almost suddenly, from an attack of
apoplexy. It is a real grief to me. I feel that I have
buried my childhood with her. She had the old souvenirs
of bygone days, and all the free and easy ways of the
good old times, with that right of loving bluntly which
one earns by six and thirty years of a life of faithful and
tender devotion. I held to her funeral being respectable,
like that of an aged relative or friend. All our family
were present, and I was greatly moved by the eagerness that
our friends showed in doing honour to a poor *bonne*. I
trust that God has found her worthy of eternal rest in Him.
Simple souls have easy ways to salvation. This poor
girl arrived in Paris from the depths of Silesia to find
a Catholic family in place of the one she had left; she
becomes a convert, puts her whole heart into loving
a little child who becomes a priest, receives Holy Communion several times from his hands, and finally the
last Sacraments on her death-bed. There is something
grand and sweet in it all, even to the *minutiæ* of the
details, which shows the kind hand of God."

The energy of his will, or rather of the faith which strengthened it, enabled the Abbé Perreyve now to undertake and carry on a life of active ministry that amazed his friends. But this was his special apostolate, this was the lesson he was to teach his generation—the power of the will to command and sustain the body under prolonged suffering and chronic ill health, the example of a life-long struggle in which the spirit, even when beaten, remained triumphant. He was justified in speaking confidently, as he did, of this power of the soul to bear up the weak vessel of clay, for he was himself a living, we might say a miraculous, witness of it. In his "Journée des Malades," he says : " The soul carries the body, and makes it live and breathe as it wills. . . . Happy the souls whom this passion (love of work) possesses to the exclusion of all others. . . . The joys of works—I speak of Christian work, accomplished with . sacrifice—done unto God, under His eye, and in His company, who shall describe them? Such work, con- quered in the first instance over the repugnance of the body, is not long in turning to a remedy."

Alas ! he used the remedy with too little discretion, and it killed him. He was charged with teaching catechism in the Church of Ste. Clothilde, a labour specially delightful to him, but severely trying to his wounded lungs. Over and above the ordinary work of his ministry, in the confessional, his attendance on the sick, and his writing, he was in constant demand for

preaching, addressing meetings of young men, etc. . . .
He was borne through the winter, however, without any
break-down, and this impunity nerved him for fresh
efforts.

"What a perpetual struggle life is!" he exclaimed,
when a truce in the battle sent him to recruit himself at
Eaux Bonnes; "nothing without fighting, everything at
the cost of blood! It is frightful, but how beautiful it is,
too! Why should such strength and ardour have been
given to souls, if they were never to fight? Let us feel
towards the struggle like good soldiers, who hold it a
grievance to be badly placed in battle, and grow impatient
for action."

This military instinct, which makes such a common
bond between the priest and the soldier, prompted the
Abbé Perreyve to apply for the post of chaplain to the
troops going to China. God, however, had a mission for him
nearer home for which his gifts more especially adapted
him. We get a glimpse of the life he was now leading
from a letter to a near relative, written on New-Year's
Day (1861): ". . . It seems that you are angry with a
certain unfortunate chaplain of the Lycée St. Louis, late
Vicar at St. Thomas d'Aquin, who has to preach, write
books, direct a college, hear confessions, and is, in fact,
so overpowered with work, that he is often days and
days without embracing his father or mother, and who
has not even the time to be ill. And I hear that you
reproach this wretched man with not writing letters!

. . . It is quite true that I have been installed chaplain
to a great college. It is far too mighty a charge for me;
but it was laid upon me, so to speak, by the Cardinal.*
I was for a long time a pupil of this Lyceum, a circumstance which they are in hopes may incline the hearts of
the young ones towards me."

These hopes were not belied. The Abbé Perreyve
possessed in a rare degree that "gift of prophecy" which
St. Paul places first amongst the gifts of the Holy Spirit,
and which he describes as the power of speaking to
every man in his own tongue. All men understood
him; the cultivated student, the unlettered workman,
the little child. Each, as he listened, saw the "secrets
of his heart made manifest," and fell down and believed.
The potency of this divine gift was nowhere so strikingly
displayed as in the sway which it exercised over that
most critical and exacting of audiences, the youth of the
Paris Lyceums. The secret of his power lay in a great
measure in the reverence which he had for these young
souls, in the timid respect with which he approached
them. Père Gratry relates a characteristic incident of one
of the conferences at the Lycée St. Louis: ". . . The
subject was one of the most delicate that words can deal
with. It was only a narrative. He related a death that
he had witnessed, and the crime which had led thereto.
Those who heard that story will remember it all their
lives. They will never forget the gentle and innocent

* Cardinal Morlot.

victims; two creatures, killed by one of those crimes
which our laws do not reach, which those of America
can and do. And when he cried out, 'Yet this man, it
appears, is a well-bred man, a gentleman with a fine
sense of honour; who knows? perhaps even a religious
man!—Messieurs, will this be your honour? is this the
religion you profess?"—there followed one of those
effects that thrill to the very centre of souls. Tears
flowed from the eyes of these young men, and when he
had done, many drew near and said to him, '*Merci,
Monsieur*, you have enlightened us for ever!'"

His influence over the turbulent young population of
Ste. Barbe was equally powerful. The director of the
college requested him to give a conference every other
Sunday morning. The arrangement retarded by half
an hour the departure of the boys to their homes, and
those who know anything of boys will commiserate the
preacher who came to address them under such circumstances. The audience, aggrieved and sullen, numbered,
between the grand college and the preparatory school,
nearly one thousand, when the Abbé Perreyve stood up
to address them. He had not, however, spoken five
minutes when their grievance disappeared; they listened
with interest, finally with delight, and two days later they
wrote to the Prefect, entreating him to let them have a
conference every Sunday, instead of every fortnight.
"Perhaps," concluded the letter, "the health and multi-
tudinous occupations of M. l'Abbé Perreyve may prevent

him acceding to our desire; but, come what may, he has earned a right to count on the gratitude that we owe him for his devotedness, and for an eloquence so remarkable in itself and so sympathetic to youth."

Here follow the signatures.

His sermons in the church of the Sorbonne met with the same enthusiastic response from an audience composed of the most distinguished men in Paris. M. de Montalembert, coming out one day from one of those impassioned discourses, hurried to the preacher's house, and being denied admittance, left a card at his door with these words in pencil: "My friend, they won't let me in; but I want to tell you that I am moved, enchanted, as I have never been, since, twenty years ago, he whose worthy successor you are inebriated my youth at Notre Dame."

But this flame, which communicated itself to all who approached him, was consuming the lamp in which it burned. There was no concealing the fact—the days of the young priest were numbered. He was named professor at the Sorbonne, with a chair of ecclesiastical history in the Faculty of Theology, to which heavy addition to his work he thus playfully alludes: "How are your good nuns? My firm belief is, that they have more sound theology in their little finger than I in my square cap of Doctor of the Sorbonne. Beg their prayers for a poor priest who fusses a great deal, but does very little good work."

"I have met with more success at the Sorbonne than I should have ventured to hope for," he says by-and-by; " the hall is full, and my audience give even too much of that intoxicating reward, applause. But it is sad enough too. How long will they applaud? Whom did they applaud last in this chair, and whom will they applaud next? If this were the sole aim of life, alas! what a pitiable recompense for the vigils and labours and efforts of a year would a momentary thrill be. . . ."

Although he owned to a sense of alarming exhaustion, he continued without a single break in his enormous accumulation of work to the close of the scholastic year. "I have been able to carry on my lectures at the Sorbonne," he says, "and to preach frequently, and the number of young men gathering round me has increased very much. Their confidence confounds me. I only hope it may contribute in some little degree to God's glory."

Like Frederic Ozanam, Henri Perreyve exercised, indeed, a marvellous fascination over the minds and the hearts of the young, his own youth establishing a kind of equality which removed all barriers to perfect sympathy; but the true key to his power was the love he bore them, the deep respect he felt for the beauty of their souls, and his burning desire to win them to their own salvation. This thirst for souls was perhaps not sufficiently controlled by prudence, for he squandered with reckless prodigality the little stock of strength which, discreetly hoarded, might have carried him safely to middle age.

No doubt the demand made upon him was great, and it was hard to resist it. "The work of ten priests was thrust upon him," says Père Gratry. "I said to him, 'But why do you not refuse all these things?' 'I am always refusing,' was his reply. And so he was; but when he had refused five or seven times, the work of five or three still remained to him."

Over and above his lectures at the Sorbonne, work in itself enough to keep him fully occupied, and this daily work of three or five priests, he was producing an incredible amount of literary work.*

Those who saw him thus prodigal of himself, were urgent in entreaty and remonstrance. Père Gratry wrote to him one morning : "My child, I cannot keep silent. I feel it my duty to warn you—to save your life, perhaps. It was agreed eight months ago—by the advice of the doctor—that you should take complete rest for several years. You know this is the steady conviction of Père Lacordaire. What has he not said about it to yourself! If, in spite of your friends, you persist in the life you are

---

* During the seven years of his priesthood he published : "Méditations sur le Chemin de la Croix ;" "La Journée des Malades ; " "Les Lettres du Père Lacordaire à des Jeunes Gens ;" with a beautiful preface. " Les Entretiens sur l'Eglise Catholique," being the substance of his lectures at the Sorbonne, Ste. Barbe, and the Lycée St. Louis. " Une Station à la Sorbonne ;" "La Pologne," which was his last work, the death-cry of his soul, protesting against the triumph of tyranny and barbarism over patriotism and faith ; and a number of short essays and biographies : " Hermann de Jouffroi," "Jeanne d'Arc," " Rosa Ferrucci," etc.

leading, it will be almost a guilty blindness. You are in
danger of a relapse; who knows? perhaps within a few
weeks of it. Forgive me. It is the voice of sincere
affection that speaks in this warning. If, from imprudence, you become quite useless, or leave us before
the time, we should feel that we were all maimed."
Another Oratorian Father signed his name to this note
under that of Père Gratry.

Père Lacordaire's expostulation came to strengthen
these remonstrances. "This must not go on," he said to
Père Gratry; "he ought to have three years' rest, not
only for the body, but for the mind and the soul. If he
goes on with this active, scattered life, in the first place
it will kill him, and in the next he will not acquire the
strength and depth and greatness that God means him to
attain. Let him come and spend three years with me at
Sorèze."

But it was no use. The voice of friendship was as of
one crying in the wilderness, "In vain do ye spread nets
before the feet of those who have wings." It requires
some mightier motive than personal considerations of
health, or even of life, to induce a priest consumed with
zeal as the Abbé Perreyve was, to rest from his labours
while the power of working remains. The rest in itself
would have been exquisite enjoyment, had he been able
to conciliate it with the work. Writing to an invalid
friend just then banished on a holiday to Rome, he says:
"I guess what you must suffer in the ambulance, whilst

we are in the field . . . but, dear friend, I implore of
you, don't study.   Look and listen ; listen to the silence
of Rome, along the ruins of the Appian Way, at the
Villa Wolkonski, on the Pincio, of a morning when the
dome of St Peter's, rising afar above the mists of the dawn,
is lighted up by the first rays of the sun.   This *informs*
the soul for the rest of one's life. . . . Lounge about,
then, and let your thoughts wander through the ages ; it
is easy enough to do this in Rome."   But these dreamy
wanderings were a luxury in which the writer himself was
not to indulge.   His constant prayer was, "Lord, give
me strength to work !"

The year 1864 opens with these words written in his
memorandum : "Never complain of fatigue when God
sends us a soul to console. . . . Pray to God to increase
my courage and leave me my sufferings. . . . Ask
God to give me back life and strength if I am to do
good to souls and to serve His glory; otherwise let
things go their way."

He had come almost to the end of his strength, when
he was requested to give a course of conferences to the
pupils of Ste. Barbe—that indocile, but ardent young audience whose sympathies he had so quickly gained and now
firmly held.   He consented at once.   He had refused
everything else this year.   "But as for the conference
at Ste. Barbe," he said to Père Gratry, "if I knew they
were to kill me the day the last one was delivered, I
should accept them all the more readily.   Any non-

commissioned officer does the same when he is ordered to a post of danger." There was no gainsaying the justice of this argument; but the fictitious strength which the effort evoked, enticed him to undertake others less imperative and sustaining. His lectures at the Sorbonne were exhausting him utterly; he knew this, but it did not induce him to give them up. "You are wearing yourself out," said a brother-in-arms, who met him one morning coming out from a lecture. "Well," was the quiet rejoinder, "and what is a priest good for but to be worn out?"

The most severe trial which ill-health had brought him so far, was compelling him to leave the Oratory. This step, which had long been foreseen as unavoidable, had been postponed to the very last; but it failed to induce the worn-out worker to take the rest which, even then, might have postponed the evil day. His sufferings increased with his weakness; but this only fanned the flame of his soul. "Suffering!" he exclaims, writing from his lonely room, scarcely now a home, in the midst of the great city; "suffering! How strange that we must always come back to this, whilst every aspiration, every instinct of our nature tends towards a happiness of which it seems almost unjust to deprive us. And what a strange contradiction to so many elements and beginnings of happiness in us. We feel so strongly, so surely, that happiness is close to us—only a step, and it would be ours! But no, there comes that grain of dust, that poverty, that nothing-at-all which spoils everything, and throws us back into the miseries of a heart betrayed. . . . All would be irreparable but for our eternal hopes; without this there would be nothing left but anguish and indignation. But we know that there lies in wait for us, after this season of struggle and trial, a substantial and blessed reality, which will be peace, understanding, perfect union, and the certainty of possession without decay and without end. Let us learn to wait, to be courageous, and to merit what we hope for.

He was now so alarmingly ill, that after the water cure the doctor ordered him South for the winter. The separation from his friends and the enforced inaction were a severe trial; but he bore it uncomplainingly.

"They say I am pretty well," he writes on New Year's Eve. "The other day the doctor—a worthy man—after examining me, sat down and said, 'Oh! since Eaux Bonnes, it has made progress; decidedly it has made progress.' I, believing that he alluded to the progress of the disease, replied very cordially, 'My dear sir, I thank you for your frankness; I had much rather know the truth at once.' The poor man bounded on his chair, and protested that the progress was in an opposite direction, which I was willing to believe; but he kept on repeating, with his Béarnais accent, 'What do you take me for? Do you think I would tell you the truth if it had been unpleasant?' It was a comical scene, and shows, as you perceive, that there are two meanings to the word progress, according as we apply it to good or evil; a luminous distinction, and as simple as it is necessary."

The exile hailed the year 1865 with a tender invocation to the Consoler of the afflicted : "Virgin most blessed. . . . Cast a glance of pity on those who are suffering, struggling. . . . Have pity on those who love and are separated ! Have pity on the isolation of our hearts ! Have pity on the weakness of our Faith ! Have pity on the objects of our tenderness ! Have pity on those who weep, on those who pray, on those who tremble. . . . Ask for all hope and peace."

From afar, he watched over the souls confided to him. " I bless you, madame, for so generously taking on yourself the care of those two poor souls. . . . Do not abandon B——. She is in danger. Alone in the world, and with her heart ! . . . You will find the remedy to vain and imaginary sorrows in charity, and devotion to the alleviation of real misery. People who suffer from the ideal should lodge near a hospital, and when their heart is bruised and overful, they should cross the street and go into the cancer ward, or the ward of chronic diseases, or the ward of the amputated. I speak from experience when I declare this to be a sovereign remedy."

As Lent drew near, his longing to resume the active functions of the ministry increased, and a wail of regret, too resigned to be called a lamentation, escapes the captive now and then. "It would be false if I pretended that the approach of Lent is not filling me with sorrow," he writes from Pau to the chaplain of Ste. Barbe. "I had hoped that a return of strength might have enabled me to make a bold venture; but it is too clear that my health would not bear the brunt of the battle, and that I must linger on sorrowfully in the ambulance. Will you convey my regrets to the directors of Ste. Barbe? . . . I say nothing to that dear *jeunesse*, whom God confided to me for a while. I feel too keenly the strength of such bonds; for I own to you that this is to me a real grief, just as the greatest joy I ever knew was being able to address those young fellows. I desire with all my heart that my successor may inherit the sympathy they gave me, and nothing would be more painful to me than to think that their kindness towards me should prove a difficulty in the way of the priest who is to address them this year. That is not the kind of success I aspired to in speaking to them of God; and I hope and trust that, while remaining true to a souvenir most precious to me, they will welcome my successor as they welcomed me. You have often seen how the reception I met with at Ste. Barbe revived my courage and renewed my failing strength. Everything is in that for the poor man who speaks, and it is in truth the audience that makes the discourse."

A month later, he says: "The thought of my dear Ste. Barbe leaves me no rest. It is a something that goes from the head to the heart, and back again. My doctor can't understand this, and I forgive him. He is not a priest, and never preached three Lents at Ste. Barbe, with the prospect of a fourth."

He was now hard at work on "La Pologne," which was to be sold for the benefit of the poor Poles whose cause he had so deeply at heart. This was his death-song. His strength was waning rapidly, and when the spring came, with the leaves and flowers that he loved, the sands were fast running down. They took him to Epinay at the beginning of April, and he spent a few weeks with his father and mother, and that sister whom he called the tutelary angel of his life. "I am very tired," he writes from the midst of them in May; "I can hardly hold my pen. . . . My friends are beginning a novena for me after to-morrow, to end on Ascension Day. Adieu! storms and sunshine, clouds, blue skies, and songs of birds. . . . Poor little speck of this world, struggling to protest that it is not heaven, but that it awaits that eternal day, of which here and there it catches a stray prophetic beam !"

The end of the novena brought new peace, but not the gift which had been asked for. The dying man spent long hours in his room alone, communing with God. He was too weak to bear for any length of time the society even of those dearest and most congenial to him; but at his lowest ebb he could rise up to meet a soul that needed him. One day, a pupil from the

military school of St. Cyr came to Epinay and knocked
at his door. It opened at once; the intruder was one of
those young men who had gathered round the Abbé
Perreyve at Ste. Barbe, and now came to make his confession.

This was the last sacramental function his old professor performed. A few days later, he was taken back
to Paris. No notable change occurred until the middle
of June, when a long fainting fit, of which he himself
knew nothing, caused great alarm to those about him.
The Abbé Bernard, a life-long friend, and his brother
almoner at the Lycée St. Louis, was sent to warn M.
and Mme. Perrevye that the danger was now imminent.
Mme. Perreyve, who was detained at her husband's
sick-bed, charged the Abbé Bernard with the solemn
mission of announcing the truth to her beloved son.

He tells us himself how the mission was fulfilled :
" However strong a soul may be, it is a hard and painful
task to bring it suddenly face to face with death; but I
was resolved to do my duty as a priest and a friend, and
I went straight to the Abbé Perreyve's room. It was at
a moment when he was suffering from great exhaustion ;
and he said, on seeing me, ' Only a few minutes to-day,
my dear friend.' A few minutes ! It was very little to
announce so grave a truth. But I called up my courage,
and began by stating very distinctly that the disease had
made alarming progress within the last two weeks. To
every word I said, however, he had a reassuring answer,

which betrayed a confidence I could not share. I prayed
God interiorly to come to my help; He sent me this
help through the sick man himself, who, becoming
suddenly affected, said to me, without anything in our
previous remarks having led to it—

"'One of the things I feel most in going away, is
having to leave you alone in life.'

"I wept with him, but I had strength to add, 'My
dear friend, since you speak to me so openly, I must tell
you that we have now cause for most serious anxiety
about you.'

"He looked at me simply and said, 'You think so?'

"'Yes, this is our impression; you had a very alarming fainting fit this morning.'

"'Ah? You surprise me; I thought I was very ill, but
not so near death. It is well; so much the better; then
you must give me Extreme Unction.'

"'That is what I was thinking of. Whom do you
wish me to ask to do you this service?'

"'You, of course—only you must let Charles know;
I want him to be present at this great act of my life.'

"'He is outside, waiting for the issue of our conversation.'

"'Ah!'—with a look of surprise—'then let it be done
at once.'"

Père Charles Perraud came in, and the Abbé Perreyve
clasped him in a long embrace. M. l'Abbé Bernard hurried
off to fetch the holy oils from St. Sulpice—St. Sulpice,

where as children the friends had prayed side by side, where they had made their First Communion, where they had been ordained, and whence one of the three now went for the last succour for the brother who was being taken from them. Just as he returned, Père Gratry arrived. The dying man, weak as he was, had risen, and dressed himself carefully, wearing only his soutane, as if he were going to say Mass and clothe himself in the sacerdotal vestments. He then passed into an adjoining room, where an altar had been prepared.

"This was the last time I saw him standing up," says Père Gratry; "he had known for about an hour that he was condemned to death. I see him still, energetic and gracious as ever. 'I am full of peace, Father; full of peace,' he said to me, smiling. While I live I will keep that picture in my heart: that soutane worn with such an air of proud joy, that noble bearing, that blanched face, those dilated dark eyes with their large, tender glance, and those last words, 'full of peace.'"

The last beautiful rite was performed, the anointed Christian joining in the responses with seraphic fervour, like one standing at the gates of pearl, not in fear but in humble exultation. Before receiving the Holy Viaticum, the Abbé Bernard asked him to make his profession of faith, as it is customary for a dying priest to do, and he recited the *Credo* in a clear voice, without faltering and with deep emotion. Then making a sign that he wished to speak, he said: "I ask pardon of my parents—whose absence I bitterly deplore at this moment—for any pain I have ever caused them. I ask pardon of my friends f⌐r the faults they have seen me commit; I thank them for their constant affection, and I beg of them to continue to pray for me long after my death. Let them not say, as too many do, and too quickly, 'He is in heaven.' Let them pray much and long for me, I implore of them ! And you, my servant, Theodore, I beg your pardon for all the scandal I have . given you; you have seen me closely; it is a bad way for men to be seen; I commend myself to your prayers."

The *Te Deum* was then recited, and the Viaticum administered. When the Abbé Perreyve had received the Body of the Lord, his face shone with a celestial brightness. He remained wrápt in God during his thanksgiving, and when it was terminated, he said to the Abbé Bernard, " *You can't conceive what a state of interior joy I am in since you told me I was going to die !* "

The Archbishop of Paris came the next day to see him. The moment his Grace entered the room, and before he could prevent it, the dying man raised himself from the bed, on which he lay dressed in his soutane, and flung himself on his knees to receive the blessing.

Friends came in numbers to bid him farewell, to ask his prayers and a last word of counsel. He was touched with grateful surprise by these proofs of tender affection ; but though he responded to them with thankful love, it was easy to see that his soul was already dwelling above all earthly ties, and yearning to be left to undisturbed communion with God. His old friend and brother, Père Adolphe Perraud, came to see him, exclaiming with tears, "I come to bid you farewell, Henri!"

"Ah!" replied Henri, "we shall not cease to work together for the cause of God and His Church—shall we? I ought to be greatly troubled because of my sins, and yet I am full of peace. Before we part, give me your blessing."

"With all my heart," replied Père Perraud, "but on condition that you give me yours."

They blessed one another, each kissing the consecrated hands of the other, and then parted; never to meet again in this world.

The Abbé Perreyve had said, when he first felt that death was advancing towards him, though he knew not how fast, "As I have always done everything quickly in my life, so I hope through the goodness of God to be able to die quickly." God was kind to him in this as in everything else.

To the last he retained the *élan* which had given to his soul, to his whole life, the impetus of a bird on the wing. It was a grand holocaust, the sacrifice of his young life that he was about to make with this same generous *élan*. He had meant to do such great things with it! "To do something for God and souls" had been a thirst with him, as with other men to achieve fortune and position, and all things had conspired to promise him the fulfilment of his noble ambition. "Our country is lost unless it returns to the faith . . . and you, my child, are called to work at this regeneration," wrote Lacordaire ; and Henri Perreyve answered to the call with the enthusiasm of a crusader. None of us can, probably, form an idea of what it must have been to such a soul, sent forth on such a mission, magnificently endowed for it, to be suddenly arrested, and ordered away from the plough just as the smoke began to ascend from the fresh-made furrows. He did not see—this was what made the sacrifice—that he had already sown the seed, and that a harvest would be gathered by those who came after him.

Three days after he had received the last Sacraments he lapsed into a silence so deep and solemn that those friends, who hovered round his death-bed, knew not how to interpret it. Had that perfect peace, which the Viaticum had brought with it, passed away to be followed by the taste of the bitterness of death ? Was the soldier, struck down in his youthful ardour, casting a look of regret on the battle-field that he was leaving too soon ? The Abbé Bernard had seen many a brave and faithful soul pass through the Valley of the Shadow, and he feared that his friend was suffering from one of those temptations against which the bravest are not always proof. He questioned him. "No," replied the dying

man, "God in His mercy still keeps me in the same
state of resignation to His will; but I own to you it
was a disappointment and a pang to me not to have
died when you told me I was going to die. Now
and then the fear comes to me that my patience may
fail if this state of waiting lasts much longer. Oh! how
I bless God now for having given me a simple faith
that goes straight to Jesus Christ, and is summed up
in that one word of His Agony, *Fiat!* . . . When my
heart is heavy, I repass in spirit the grand platonic ideas
of Eternal Beauty, and thus philosophy, too, helps me
in its turn, and brings me back to piety."

Thus the Eternal Beauty, whose worship had been
the key-note of his life, came to soften with its divine
rays the parting struggle of the soul that was about to
enter its presence. On the feast of Corpus Christi,
to which he had a special devotion, he was lying on
his bed, dressed, when the Abbé Bernard came in, and,
at his request, read to him the eighth chapter of the
Epistle to the Romans, that he had always loved, and
used to meditate upon at the foot of the Cross in the
Coliseum. When they came to the thirtieth verse, "*And
whom He predestinated, them He also called; and
whom He called, them He also justified; and whom He
justified, them He also glorified,*" the Abbé Bernard
looked up to see what impression these words—which
moved him deeply—had made upon his friend. Their
eyes met; both were full of tears. The reader went on.

Each sentence flooded their souls with a new and fuller emotion. Like the disciples on the road to Emmaus, Jesus was with them, and made their hearts burn within them at the inspired words. When they came to the last verse, " Neither life, nor death, nor angels, . . . nor things present, nor things to come, . . . nor any creature, shall be able to separate us from the love of God," their hearts brimmed over, they sobbed aloud, and pressed each other's hands.

"Leave me alone with God," said the Abbé Perreyve, after a long silence. Then, as his friend was leaving the room, he called out, "Stay! bring me Holy Communion first." The Abbé Bernard brought it to him, and withdrew, full of awe, as from the presence of a great mystery.

They thought he would have gone home that night ; but he did not, and again gently expressed his disappointment, adding quickly an act of conformity to the Divine will. "I represent to myself the will of God under the form of a citadel on a high rock," he said to Père Charles Perraud : "here I take refuge, and I say, 'I know nothing but this.'"

But though the delay seemed long to his impatient soul, the end was very near. On Sunday evening the Sister who was watching him saw symptoms which made her fear for the night. The next morning his father and mother were sent for.

Meantime the Abbé Bernard, who had celebrated

Mass for him at daybreak, came in and said he would not leave him, but remain by his bedside, or in the next room.

"Am I much worse?" inquired his friend, calmly.

"Perhaps you may wish to confess, or to receive Communion ; besides, I promised the Sister not to leave you till she returned."

"Ah! I understand. Then it is to be for to-day. We must make ready for the great combat. Go at once and bring me the Viaticum." He remained alone for a long thanksgiving.

His father and mother arrived later in the day. The moment he saw them entering the room, he called out, "We must take courage! Love is strength ; God above all! It is He who upholds in this hour of anguish; I know it more than ever at this hour."

They knelt beside him and he blessed them; he, their son, but also the Lord's anointed. Then he asked the Sister for the crucifix, that he might kiss it.

"Give me yours," he said, "not my own; yours that has been pressed by so many dying lips."

Presently he said to his mother, " If I die to-morrow, it will be the anniversary of my First Communion."

"Dear child," answered the mother through her tears, " I was very happy that day!"

"Well, and you must be happy to-morrow, too," was the reply.

He then called his sister to him, and told her of some

changes that were to be made in the family vault, and in
a clear, unfaltering voice dictated his epitaph to her:
"Satiabor cum apparuerit gloria Tua." (Ps. xvi. 15.)

After this his agony may be said to have begun; but
consciousness remained unclouded, and the soul in
full possession of itself. He held the crucifix, pressing
it to his lips with tender invocations: "Come quickly,
my Lord! . . . Soon, Jesus, soon."

He was as peaceful as a child in its mother's arms,
and the mourners who knelt round him felt moved
rather to give thanks than to grieve at this blessed going
home of their beloved one. The afternoon wore on;
the long shadows of the summer evening gathered in
the death-chamber.

Towards seven o'clock the dying man suddenly made
an effort to raise himself on his pillow; his face grew
livid, his large, dark eyes fixed themselves with an
expression of terror on some object present, but visible
only to him, and he cried out twice, in a strong voice,
"*I am afraid! I am afraid!*" The Abbé flew to his
side.

"Don't be afraid of God," he said; "cast yourself into
the arms of His mercy. *In te, Domine, speravi.*"

The other looked at him and said, "It is not God
I am afraid of. Oh no! I am afraid . . . *that they
won't let me die!*"

They gave him the crucifix to kiss—Père Lacordaire's
crucifix, that he had had all day—and the Abbé Bernard

pronounced slowly the words, " My God, I love Thee with all my heart, for time and for eternity."

" *Oh yes . . . with all my heart!*" repeated his friend, imprinting a long kiss upon the wounded feet of his Saviour. These were his last words. He grew oppressed; his breath came fast and thick; by degrees the breathing became faint, then inaudible; the shades of death closed round him, and Henri Perreyve faded into life.

COUNSELS TO THE SICK.

COUNSELS TO THE SICK.

SICKNESS CONSIDERED AS A WARNING.

SICKNESS withdraws a man from the world, and warns him to turn his thoughts to that life which is the only true life. Many things conspire to hinder us from thinking of eternity, but none, perhaps, more dangerously than what the Evangelist calls the *pride of life*—that proud sense of life and energy which too often lures us on until we reach the very brink of the grave, when awakening comes too late.

From the first moment of our awaking, worldly affairs fill our thoughts. We rise refreshed for the day's work. Letters and newspapers lie ready to our hand and furnish topics of varied interest. We eat and drink heartily, and feel full of strength and vital energy. We turn at once to whatever our business may be, and give all our thoughts and attention to it. Things are going prosperously with us, our diligence brings its own reward, and our ship sails triumphantly down the stream of life.

The day is too short for all we have to do, but when it is over, we join our family circle and give ourselves up to domestic happiness, or it may be we go in search of pleasure in some less quiet form. Night closes in, we lie down to rest, and sleep drops a veil over the work and amusements of another day.

During sleep, the blood is calmed and cooled ; the vital principle is strengthened and renewed, the body rests. But when does the soul rest ? How many hours do we devote to its renewal ?

Alas ! the whirlwind of life sweeps us on with it, and we have become so accustomed to the rapid pace that the least check startles us and creates a feeling of alarm, such as a man experiences who, being run away with in a carriage, wakes up to find it standing still. We expect the stream of life to flow on high and free between its banks, with vessels passing up and down, freighted with men and things from distant lands ; we must have our interest kept up by shifting scenes, by the farewells of those who are setting sail, and the glad greetings of new arrivals ; we must have sunshine to make joy and victory brighter, and shade

to hide every ruin ; above all, we must have novelty
and unceasing movement. If in the midst of this
prosperous career any one ventures in the name
of religion to turn the thoughts of the happy man
from the gay scene of this world, and to remind
him that true life consisteth not in the present,
but in the life of the world to come, the warning
is received with surprise or indifference ; the messenger is looked on as a kill-joy, a gloomy fanatic,
and his words fall unheeded to the ground.

The children of God are not always free from
this delusion. They have the words of Holy
Scripture and the teaching of the Church to warn
and protect them, and twice at least every day
God takes them by the hand in the silence of
prayer ; but they are often too careless to profit
as they ought by these warnings. The spirit is
borne down by the weight of the flesh, the salutary
fear of death is stifled by the thrilling consciousness
of health and strength, and the whisperings of
grace are silenced. But, as the unsteady gaze
of the drunken man, who sees the stars moving,
does not affect the course of the heavenly bodies,
so neither does the intoxication of the soul, hurry-
ing on to death, bewildered by pleasure and
business, change that eternal goal whither she is
tending, or that judgment which awaits her there.
Whether we sleep or wake on our road, the journey
will come to an end, and we shall find ourselves

some day at that bourne where dreams are dis-
pelled by the unchangeable realities of eternity.
Who among us dares to say that it will be time
enough then to awake, or that it will not be a
terrible thing to appear before Him whom Bossuet
calls the "Reasonable God," whilst we are still
plunged in the slough of passion and giddy with
the wine of this world's delights?

I know not what the sinner thinks of this, when
he is forced to think of it, but I know that the
thought has made the saints tremble.

Is it not, then, a manifest mercy to each one
of us, an act of adorable compassion, when Divine
Providence sends sickness to check a soul in the
midst of this infatuation, and withdraw it for a
time into the presence of eternity, and the companionship of suffering which has such power to
make the body turn itself to the soul, and the soul
to God?

It cost you a hard struggle in the days of your
health and strength to turn aside from the world,
and draw nearer to God. It needed superhuman
strength to enable you to break loose even for a
while from the chains, so terribly potent and
fascinating, which bound you to the things of
earth, to put them out of your thoughts, and
snatch a quiet hour for meditation and prayer.
But now your soul is no longer bewildered by
the rush of life and the exhilarating sense of youth

and health. Your bodily energies are brought
low, and the pride of that beauty which was the
object of so much care, and the instrument of so
many perilous delusions is humbled. Your physician has prescribed silence. Obey his order, and
make those around you obey it ; God intends
that it should be beneficial to your soul. Recollections of your past life will crowd upon you during
long sleepless and unoccupied hours ; do not drive
them away.

Look back through the course of your days,
and compare them one with another. Which have
been your really happy days? Those well-remem-
bered ones when you performed some good action,
when you made some sacrifice to God, or those
others when you ran after your own pleasures?
Is it not true that in proportion as you have
forgotten God, the warmth has died out of your
life ? Go back to the innocent days of your
childhood, to the undying memory of your First
Communion, to the first aspirations which consecrated your soul to the Divine Friend. Where
has this Guest been since you drove Him from
you ? You fancy, perhaps, that He has been far
away ? You are mistaken. He has been close
to you. He is there, knocking at the door of your
heart; He has been there all the time that you
have been forgetting Him ; He has foreseen this
hour that has come to you, this season of silence

and recollection; He has been patiently waiting like a beggar at a king's gate. He, the King of kings, has stood at your door, waiting. *Waiting on you!* He waits, He cries out, He entreats. His voice has at last made itself heard. Take care, now, that you despise it not. "To-day, if you shall hear His voice, harden not your hearts." *

And you, faithful ones, whom sickness has not found enslaved in the bonds of the world, the flesh, and the devil, receive it, nevertheless, as a special grace, and prepare yourselves to profit by it. You have the faith, but has your life been always in conformity with what it commands? Your soul may not have fallen asleep amidst the allurements of the senses, but has she not to some extent succumbed to that spiritual torpor from which the hand of God alone can arouse us? Have you not lost that perfect peace which belongs only to a pure conscience and a heart stayed on God? Have you held yourself detached from temporal things, and kept the eye of your soul steadily fixed on things eternal? Look into your conscience.

God calls you for a while into closer communion with Him. Accept humbly and thankfully the suffering that is sent by His loving kindness to purify you and draw you into converse with His divine Heart. You will thus profit by the salutary

* Psalm xciv. 8.

chastisement, and by-and-by you will be able to see that it was a blessing, and you will find the days too short that have been so blest to you.

The joy of the reaper is measured by the sweat with which he waters the grain as he drops it into the open furrow.

On First Waking.

The Sick Man. O God, Thou art my God, early will I seek Thee. Lord, be Thou my help from the first dawn of day, for Thou knowest that even from the beginning my strength faileth me, and that I shrink from the long hours of pain that I see before me. Time was when I awoke always with gladness, for I felt that each returning dawn brought me nothing but joy. This was in the days of my childhood, and life was a happy mystery that I was impatient to unravel. My mother's kisses opened my eyes, the world was full of promise; I believed in happiness, I knew nothing of care or sorrow. Lord, as time went on, I learned to think differently. Thou hast taught me that he who has not suffered understands nothing, and in order that I may not be one of these, Thou hast laid me on this bed of suffering, where the hours are heavy as lead and slow as a passing bell.

Lord, wilt Thou not bear with me if I complain

to Thee awhile? This burden that falls upon me
when I awake is terrible. I know so well what the
day has in store for me—the wearing pain that
nothing seems to relieve, and which, like some
pitiless torturer, is deaf to all entreaties, never
gives me a moment's respite—the same enforced
inaction, more fatiguing than the hardest work.
Then there is the distress and anxiety of those
nearest and dearest to me, far more trying than
any other pain. I shall have to listen with a
cheerful countenance to foolish, commonplace condolences, and to assent with apparent belief to
assurances which I know to be perfectly untrue.
There will be the same remedies to repeat, ex-
periments to undergo which have been tried over
and over again in vain, and which make me suffer
in anticipation more even than in reality.

I shall have to hear all day from my sick bed
the laughter of people in rude health passing and
repassing under my window, while I am shut up,
a prisoner, unable to move. All this comes before
me the moment I awake to consciousness, and
therefore it is that my waking is a moment full of
dull pain and bitterness. But I will not murmur,
my God, for this trial is like a goad, urging my soul
to turn at once from myself to Thee and throw
herself into Thy merciful arms. My heart will try
to be submissive and offer itself to Thee at the
morning's dawn, before the labourer has gone forth

to his toil, and before the night-watch has left his post. O God! hear my cry, and turn Thy face towards me, for Thou alone art my strength, and I have only Thee to look to for help in the long day that opens before me.

The Comforter. My son, remember those words which I spoke to the chief of My Apostles, " When thou wast younger thou didst gird thyself, and didst walk where thou wouldst : but when thou shalt be old, thou shalt stretch forth thy hands, and another shall gird thee, and lead thee whither thou wouldst not." * In these words is set forth the mystery of My union with the soul ; they call her to the highest degree of confidence in Me of which she is capable, to that supreme and perfect act which consists in entire self-abandonment. These words were not spoken to My servant until I had three times proved the depth of his love, and had three times received from his mouth the promise of persevering faithfulness ; by this thou mayest see that they are not to be listened to lightly, and that it is only to faithful and chosen souls that I address them.

" When thou wast younger " thou didst walk according to thy human will, seeking thy consolation on earth, amusing thyself with the pleasures of this world and the sweetness of life, as children amuse themselves with a toy, and cry if it is taken

* St. John xxi. 18.

from them. Then thou didst think to dispose as thou wouldst of thy days and of thy life ; liberty was the desire of thy heart. It pleased thee to forecast the order and consequence of actions, and to plan all as seemed most agreeable to thine own mind and senses. Youth and health appeared to warrant these forecastings, and nothing entered into them which could disturb the course of thy wishes. "In those days" thou didst walk whither thou wouldst. But dost thou think that the soul is called to no higher degree of perfection than this? Whither would such a proud spirit of independence lead thee, and what service could I expect from a heart given up solely to its own desires and its own selfish happiness? Doubt it not, My son, even as the vase must be broken in order that the precious ointment may be poured forth, so must the heart be broken in order that it may be enlarged and enlightened, filled with charity to man, and made fruitful in My service and to My glory. For this reason I have permitted the course of time to bring upon thee the trial of suffering and sorrow. Thou didst not need to grow old in order to learn that the dreams of childhood could not last, and that these passionate longings for liberty must be followed by that acceptable and willing obedience, which makes man an active victim in the service of God and of his fellow-men. Thou didst then begin to feel the approach of that Divine "Another"

of whom My Gospel speaks; thou didst understand that the "one thing needful" was to do, not
thine own will, but His; not to accomplish thine
own passing fancies, but to have a share in the
working out of His eternal purposes.

And who is that Divine "Another" but Myself,
thy Friend and thy Brother; Who suffered and died
for man so that not one of all thy sufferings might
be unknown to Me? Let Me, then, draw near to
thee, and order thy life. Close thine eyes, My
child, close thine eyes; stretch forth thine hands,
let Me gird thee with the girdle that I have chosen
for thee from all eternity. Whether it be a girdle
of cords, or of iron, or of fire; whether it be the
girdle of penance, of great tribulation, or of pain
and sickness, stretch forth thy hands, and let Me
gird thee with the spirit of abandonment to My
will. Nay, thou must suffer Me to lead thee
blindfold by the hand, there whither thou willest
not, and canst not will to go. What sign is there,
My child, of thy willingness to go to pain, and
loneliness and inactivity, to a life hidden from the
world, to prolonged suffering? All the instincts of
thy human nature revolt against this invitation
and recoil from entering on this thorny road. But
thou must overcome thy repugnance, and like the
little child, who walks fearlessly in the dark, holding his mother's skirt, so do thou walk through the
night of thy trials, holding My hand, and remem-

bering that My presence is light and comfort, and that he who follows Me "walketh not in darkness."

Think of this on awaking at the dawn, and let thy first act be a brave step on this road of faith and abandonment.

The Sick Man. Lord, I place my life, my body and soul, and my whole being, in Thy hands. *In manus tuas, Domine commendo spiritum meum.*

The Church Bells.

If you have ever been kept a prisoner to your sick bed on a lovely summer's morning, and have heard the bells ring out for some great festival, and seen your friends, or your family, set off to join in the joyous offices of the day; if you have watched from your window young men and maidens and little children in their Sunday clothes hastening to church, and longed in vain to leave your solitary chamber and join them, you will be able to enter into what I am now going to write.

I have loved, Lord, the beauty of Thy house: and the place where Thy glory dwelleth. From my childhood I have loved the beauty of the Lord: yes, I loved it, and sought it, and delighted in it, even whilst the beauty of this world had charms for me, and when I was still able to take a part in its pleasures. I loved Thy holy offices, the

solemn pomp of Thy worship, the austere harmony
of the psalms, the pealing of the organ, the flowers
and lights, and sweet odours of Thy sanctuary.

I loved to gaze on Thy holy altar, and see Thy
priest lift up his hands to bestow on Thy people
the blessing he received for them from Thee. I
loved that little corner, where, hid away from every
one, I was wont to kneel down and forget the
whole world to think only of Thee.

Lord, even then I loved the beauty of Thy
house. How much more do I love it now that
I am condemned to stay away from it and to
remain an exile from Thy tabernacles. Why has
my love for Thy courts been turned into bitterness? For now I dread the return of Thy festivals
instead of hailing them with delight. A feeling of
overpowering sadness comes upon me. Solitary
prayer wearies me. When I am reading the
psalms all by myself, I long for the sound of their
familiar harmonies. I grieve for all things in Thy
house. The work-a-day noises in the street sound
sadder and drearier on these festival days, all
things are harder to bear. Lord, bear with my
complaining, and cast me not from Thee in the
hour of my weakness.

The Comforter. My child, I have compassion on
thy sorrow, and the purity of thy desires touches
thy Father's heart. Thou grievest that thou art
not able to join My children and sit with them

H

at the banquet of My holy mysteries : this sorrow is a proof of thy love, and places thee in the number of those faithful servants who cannot sing the glad canticle far from Jerusalem. Blessed be thou for this faithfulness, for in these days it is rare amongst the children of men ; but let it comfort thy heart, instead of discouraging thee. Delight in the beauty of My earthly tabernacles, but remember that the outward pomp and ceremonial is only the beginning of piety, not its end. It is the religion of souls to whom I have as yet made known only a portion of My secrets, and who, being, as it were, in their spiritual infancy, need to be fed with milk, for they would not be able to bear stronger food. These I let stand in the outer courts of My temple, and give them, to aid their devotion, the allurements of sound, of rhythm, and colour, and thus I lead them to the contemplation of those mysteries which they would not be able to bear without the help of the senses. But all souls do not equally need these auxiliaries. Some, more detached from external things and human sensibility, can find My presence more easily in solitary meditation than in the midst of external rites and ceremonies.

There are many ways by which souls may be raised to this higher form of love, but none is more powerful or efficacious than sickness, when it is borne in a true spirit of submission and self-sacrifice.

Sickness separates the Christian from the world, and from all that charms the senses, and makes a great silence round him. His body is no longer a source of temptation and self-delusion, but an instrument of sacrifice and sanctification. Sickness breaks down all the obstacles which self too often raises between Me and the soul. The praise of man is no longer sought after, the spiritual gaze is turned inwards, and the soul of the suffering Christian finds itself alone with Me.

Now, if thou wilt reflect, My child, on the strenuous efforts which My saints have made to arrive at this blessed solitude, and on the complaints they have uttered about the difficulty of reaching it, even for a season, then thou wilt understand the surpassing value of this first blessing which sickness brings with it. It leads the soul to that growing spiritual worship which I announced to the woman of Samaria ; when I said to her, "The hour cometh when you shall neither on this mountain, nor in Jerusalem adore the Father. . . . The hour cometh, and now is, when the true adorers shall adore the Father in spirit and in truth. For the Father also seeketh such to adore him. God is a Spirit; and they that adore Him must adore Him in spirit and in truth." *

Temples of stone will pass, even My sacraments, which are necessary now because the state of man

* St. John iv. 21, 23, 24.

here below is not the state of angels—My sacraments will pass away, and faith, and hope shall pass away, as I have said by the mouth of My Apostle; but what will never pass away, is worship in spirit and truth, for this is perfect charity, and the soul's eternal rest in Me.

Look upon sickness, then, my child, as an initiation into the perfect religion which will one day be that of the saints in heaven. Be satisfied to have that share in My sacraments of which sickness does not deprive thee, for I have so ordered that they may be brought to thy sick bed; and do not regret overmuch that which pleased thy imagination, and gratified thy senses in My material temple. I accept thy longings, because they are pure and innocent; but let them not oppress thy heart, and remember that there is not in the whole world any temple or tabernacle so dear to Me as the soul of the just man.

THE HOLY SACRIFICE.

One grievous trial of true Christians who are kept away from Church by sickness is that they cannot join in the Sacrifice of the Mass, and they feel this privation all the more because, being reduced by suffering to the condition of victims, they have gained a higher insight into the Sacrifice of the Altar. Some go no further than these regrets, and

imagine they can have no share in the August
Sacrifice, because they cannot be present at it, and
so end by thinking nothing more about it. Thus
they altogether lose the blessing they might gain
in the time of sickness by union of intention with
the Divine Victim. These Christians do not sufficiently realize that their very weakness gives them
a direct share in the sacrifice of Jesus Christ, and
that in ascending the altar of pain and sorrow, to
which God has called them, they may there celebrate, in union with the sacrifice of the Cross and
of the Altar, another real sacrifice, by which God
may be honoured and their own salvation pro-
moted.

The suffering Christian may, in fact, apply to
himself every part of the sacrifice in a true though
figurative sense. For the doctrine of Jesus Christ
is true in many senses, and the mind of man would
lose itself in vain in trying to discover the infinite
variety of meanings that it is capable of bearing.

Mass is a sacrifice whereby the priest not only
commemorates but veritably continues the sacrifice
of the Cross, and applies the merits of the one
Eternal Victim to the wants of individual souls and
the Church universal. True to this spirit of
remembrance and continuation, which links by an
indissoluble chain each separate Mass to the first
Mass on Calvary, the Church teaches that whenever the Holy Sacrifice is offered up, three Sacri-

ficers meet in the person of the priest, represented
by him, and acting through him.

First, there is Jesus Christ, Eternal Victim and
High Priest, continuing in His priests the everlasting Priesthood which He received from His Father.
So truly present is He with His ministers that He
commands them to say, in the act of consecration,
not "This is the Body, and this is the Blood of
Christ," but in direct words, "This is *My* Body, this
is *My* Blood."

Secondly, there is the whole Catholic Church
communicating to her priests the mission she has
received from her Divine Spouse to continue the
sacrifice, and she acts and speaks through them, as
a people acts and speaks through its ambassadors.
Thus all souls who are united to the Church by
the bond of charity, join, even without knowing it,
in the oblation offered on every Altar throughout
the world, and partake of its merits.

Let us pause to consider these three points, and
we shall see the suffering Christian may, in a certain
sense, unite them in his own person.

If the first who immolates in the person of the
priest at the Altar is Jesus Christ himself, so may
we dare to say that the first who suffers in the sick
Christian is the same Jesus Christ, and that the
personal sacrifice of the faithful soul is, like the
Holy Eucharist (though in a less perfect way), a
memorial and continuation of the Sacrifice of the

Cross. This is what the Apostle means when he says, " I fill up those things that are wanting of the sufferings of Christ."* Not assuredly that Christ's Passion was incomplete, or that it needed perfecting in itself, but that, being the Sacrifice of the whole Church, it needed to be continued by a voluntary acceptance of it on the part of God's children. In every sick Christian, therefore, Christ suffers, as in every celebrant He offers Himself up. He alone gives to both sacrifices a permanent balm. He alone obtains for each oblation a blessing which shall never end.

Beware, therefore, child of God, of despising your infirmity ; for like unto those martyrs of primitive times who took the name of Christbearers, so do you also bear within you the suffering Christ, and perpetuate by your sacrifice the sacrifice of His Passion. You are too weak and too miserable, it may be, to think of your sufferings without sadness ; but turn your eyes from self, and as the priest at the altar, whilst penetrated with his own unworthiness, still recognizes in himself the presence of the spotless High Priest, so may you, clothed with the priesthood of suffering, see Christ Jesus who suffers and offers up Himself within you.

The second participator in the sacrifice of the Holy Eucharist is the Universal Church ; and she,

* Col. i. 24.

too, is to be found sharing in the sacrifice of the afflicted Christian, increasing his virtues and profiting by his sufferings. This is one of the outcomes of the beautiful doctrine of the Communion of Saints, through which we know that the same laws which rule the inner life of God, by binding the Three Persons in One Godhead, also govern the Christian community, and bind the different members of the Church in one individual Unity. Thus the same Life animates all those souls who are united to the Church by the same bond of charity. Not one of these souls can think, or love, or act, without influencing the general state of the rest; still less can any Christian suffer and the whole Church not suffer with him; nor can any fresh merit accrue to him, and the whole Church not share therein. This is also the doctrine of St. Paul, when he says, " But now there are many members indeed, yet one body. Yea, much more those that seem to be the more feeble members of the body, are more necessary. And if one member suffer anything, all the members suffer with it; or, if one member glory, all the members rejoice with it. Now you are the body of Christ, and members of member."* Nothing, then, should be farther from the thoughts of God's children, when the fire of tribulation overtakes them, than the idea of isolation. We may broadly assert that the word

* 1 Cor. xii. 20, 22, 26, 27.

isolation is not a Christian word, for a Christian is never alone, and the soul in which Divine grace dwells bears within itself the very Presence of God and of His Church. But in the case of acceptable suffering and self-sacrifice, this feeling of isolation is more especially false, and contradicts all that we know and believe respecting the mystery of the union of souls.

Know, then, suffering Christian, that as the priest does not offer the Holy Eucharist alone, nor reap the benefit of it alone, neither are you alone nor forsaken on the altar of your sufferings. The whole Church is there with you. Never imagine, then, that your sufferings are lost, or that the silent strivings of your patient love are thrown away. Do you not know that the most obscure priest who celebrates at the Altar of a remote village church, enriches from the depth of his solitude the treasure of the Church universal, and adds, so to speak, to the glories of heaven? A power something like this now belongs to you. All that you suffer is the common treasure of souls, and the revelations of the Last Day will reveal to you such and such unknown fellow Christians, whose conversion and eternal happiness you will have unconsciously obtained.

Lastly, the third sacrificer who takes part in the Holy Sacrifice is the priest himself. The Apostle says that he " offers up sacrifice first for his own sins, and then for the people's." * Hence, whatever may be the special intention for which the Holy Sacrifice is celebrated, the priest has a special share in the merits of the Victim, and, except in cases too terrible to think of, he never comes down from the Altar without having received an increase of faith and love. The law of justice ordains that whoever offers a sacrifice should profit by it; or, as it is expressed in the Ordinary, "they that serve the Altar, partake with the Altar." † Partake, then, O sufferer, of the altar of your soul. Let nothing be wasted in vain murmurings, or lamentations; let nothing lessen the fulness of the merit with which God is waiting to reward your patience.

The Apostle makes known to us in a few words the surprising greatness of this reward: "The sufferings of this time are not worthy to be compared with the glory to come, that shall be revealed to us." ‡ And again: "For that which is at present momentary and light of our tribulation, worketh for us above measure exceedingly an eternal weight of glory." §

THE HOLY SACRIFICE.—*continued.*

Having now realized the value of your sacrifice and the high dignity of your priesthood, ascend the

---

* Heb. vii. 27.   † 1 Cor. ix. 13.
‡ Rom. viii. 18.   § 2 Cor. iv. 17.

altar which God's hand has prepared for you from
all eternity, and do not hesitate to pronounce the
first words of the holy sacrifice *Introibo ad altare
Dei*, "I will go unto the altar of God."

Introit.

"I will go" up, O Lord, early in the morning,
"unto the altar" where Thou dost require at my
hands the sacrifice of my own will, and of all the
longings of my heart.

O God, Who wast the joy of my youth, Thou
canst renew it as the eagle's, and give me back all
my health and my strength, if so they may tend to
Thy glory.

"For Thou art the God of my strength, why
hast Thou cast me off? and why do I go sorrowful
whilst the enemy afflicteth me?"

"Send out Thy Light and Thy Truth," for
through them only can I be set free from all vain
and worldly desires, and be enabled to ascend without faltering the Calvary to which Thou art pleased
to call me.

"Why art thou sorrowful, O my soul? and why
dost thou disquiet me?"

"Hope in God, for I will still give praise to
Him: Who is the salvation of my countenance and
my God."

Glory be to the Father, and to the Son, and to the Holy Ghost :

As it was .in the beginning, is now, and ever shall be, world without end. Amen.

By my weakness and by my strength, by my life and by my death, may God the Holy Trinity be glorified, now and for ever. Amen.

Confiteor.

I confess to Almighty God, to the blessed Mary ever Virgin, and to all the saints, that I have deserved by my sins all the pains that I am now suffering, and that my illness is the just chastisement of my ingratitude and hardness of heart. How often have I abused my strength and health for the gratification of my caprices and sinful inclinations! How often have I put off till the morrow the accomplishment of my good resolutions, and obedience to the call of grace! How often have I presumptuously counted on length of days and the patience of a merciful God! Lord, I should still be in the midst of these vain dreams had not Thy merciful hand awakened me by suffering, and sent me this illness in order that I might think seriously of my ways, and consider the work of my salvation.

The Kyrie Eleison.

O God, look down at least with compassion on the present disposition of my heart; forget my base ingratitude, and remember only the misery and need of Thy servant!

Lord have mercy on me! Christ have mercy on me!

The Gloria in Excelsis.

Glory be to God in the highest heaven, and peace on earth to men of good will! *Peace!* Oh! my Saviour, I have learned that it is not to be found in the possession of sensible goods, but in the heart which has preserved its innocence unsullied, or regained it by repentance. I was troubled often in the pleasures of that selfish, barren life which I lived far from Thee : one thing was wanting to my happiness—peace. And lo! peace has entered into my soul by suffering, because suffering accepted brings with it order, and order breeds calm. I feel that all things are now in their right place. A God of love is no longer outraged; a sinner is mourning over his sins and expiating them : these tears and pains are reconciling practice with mercy. Oh, my Lord Jesus! I adore this, the work of Thy hands ; only make it complete by washing away from my heart all the stains that disfigured it.

Lamb of God, Who takest away the sins of the world, have mercy on me !

Oh, Thou Who sittest at the right hand of the Father, have mercy on me !

For Thou only art holy, Thou only art most high, Thou only art omnipotent, Jesus Christ with the Holy Spirit in the glory of God the Father. Amen.

The Collect.

O God, Who in teaching us to pray, has bidden us say, " Father, Thy will be done," help me from the bottom of my heart to enter into the spirit of these Divine words. Enable me to place myself entirely in Thy hands, that so I may from henceforth find all my hope and happiness in accomplishing Thine adorable and eternal will ; through Jesus Christ our Lord. Amen.

The Epistle.

" For we would not have you ignorant, brethren, of our tribulation, which came to us in Asia, that we were pressed out of measure, above our strength, so that we were weary even of life.

" But we had in ourselves the answer of death, that we should not trust in ourselves, but in God Who raiseth the dead.

" Who hath delivered and doth deliver us out of

so great dangers : in whom we trust that He will yet also deliver us."*

I have felt throughout my whole being this "sentence of death" of which the Apostle speaks, and his words show me clearly that I must not trust in this short and uncertain life, but only in Thee, the Lord of all life, Who canst, if such be Thy will, raise up even the dead from their graves.

This, then, O Lord, is often the object of that menace of death which the sick man feels in the fading away of his health and strength. Thou wouldst have him learn from this warning voice that he has not in himself the principle of life, but that he must look above and turn to God for safety. When he has duly profited by this sacred warning, Thou dost lead him back from the brink of the grave to life, and restore to him that strength which he has now learned to look upon as only lent to him by Thee. Will it be thus with me, O Lord ? I may indeed hope so, for the remembrance of Thy mercies in the past bids me hope all things in the future.

The Gospel.

"As He was speaking these things unto them, behold, a certain ruler came up, and adored him, saying : Lord, my daughter is even now dead ;

* 2 Cor. i. 8.

but come, lay Thy hand upon her, and she shall
live.

"And Jesus rising up followed him, with his
disciples. And, behold, a woman who was troubled
with an issue of blood twelve years, came behind
him, and touched the hem of his garment. For
she said within herself: If I shall only touch his
garment, I shall be healed. But Jesus turning, and
seeing her, said : Be of good heart, daughter, thy
faith hath made thee whole. And the woman was
made whole from that hour.

"And when Jesus was come into the house of
the ruler, and saw the minstrels and the multitude
making a rout, He said : Give place, for the girl is
not dead, but sleepeth. And they laughed him to
scorn. And when the multitude was put forth, he
went in, and took her by the hand. And the maid
arose. And the fame hereof went abroad into all
that country. And as Jesus passed from thence,
there followed him two blind men, crying out, and
saying, Have mercy on us, O Son of David. And
when he was come to the house, the blind men
came to him. And Jesus saith to them, Do you
believe that I can do this unto you ? They say to
him, Yea, Lord. Then he touched their eyes, saying, According to your faith be it done unto you.
And their eyes were opened, and Jesus strictly
charged them, saying, See that no man know this.
And Jesus went about all their cities and towns,

teaching in their synagogues, preaching the Gospel of the kingdom, and healing every disease and *every infirmity.*" *

Lord, how consoling to me at this moment, are, above all, the last words of this Thy Gospel! *Every infirmity.* No human suffering, however mean and pitiful, was despised by Thee during Thy mortal life, and Thou wert as full of compassion for the miseries of the body as for those of the soul. It is not so with men. Those who are readiest to exhort others to patience have often never suffered themselves, and they preach heroism all the more easily because of their little experience of pain or trial. But Thou, my Saviour, speakest as one who knows all things. Thy compassion is wide and deep enough to make room for all our infirmities. Thy Heart feels all our sorrows and comforts them. How can I ever adequately trust this Heart of Thine, so full of love and pity! Teach me to come to Thee with confidence, and pour forth to Thee the complaint which Thou wilt not despise.

The Offertory.

Lord, Thou dost not despise my sufferings, and still less wilt Thou disdain my free and willing sacrifices, whereby at this time I make myself, as it

* St. Matt. ix. 18.

were, a victim for Thine Altar, offering to Thee fully and entirely, my whole self, my body, my soul, and my spirit in acknowledgment of Thy sovereign power over me and all Thy creatures, to adore Thee as my Lord and my God, to thank Thee for all the benefits which Thou hast bestowed on me and mine, to appease thine anger which my sins have greatly provoked, and to obtain for Thy whole Church those graces and blessings of which she stands in need.

To Thee, O Lord, do I offer this sacrifice of myself and my sufferings, beseeching Thee to receive it, to bless and sanctify it, that so it may be acceptable as a sweet smelling perfume in Thy sight. In humility and contrition of heart, Lord, I offer myself to Thee as Thy victim. Grant that my sacrifice may be pleasing to Thee, my Lord and my God! Come, Holy Spirit, Almighty and Eternal God, and bless this sacrifice humbly offered for the love of Thy Holy Name.

Lavabo inter innocentes.

I will wash my hands amongst the innocent, I will compass Thy altar with love, and give Thee thanks for having purified my hands by the fire of tribulation, and for having begun the conversion of my heart. Finish Thy work, Lord; separate me from the children of this world who live for blood, and gold, and understand nothing about Thy Cross. Strengthen my soul, in silence and retreat; make my will straight and strong. Grant that when I regain my liberty, if such be Thy will, I may walk henceforth in innocence, and that my feet may never more stray from the right path, but that I may take Thy part with a fearless voice amongst the assemblies of men, and devote myself to praising and blessing Thee!

Orate Fratres.

My brethren, help me with your prayers that I may fulfil my sacrifice.

Christian, may the Lord receive the sacrifice of thy patience for the glory of His name, for thy benefit and for that of the Church universal.

The Preface.

Sursum corda! Let me no longer give way to vain complainings, nor hearken to faint-hearted counsels, nor ought which could lead me back to earthly things.

O my God, I would now fain forget myself, and losing sight of my own misery, look only at Thee. Many a soul is made desolate by dwelling on self rather than on Thee, Source of all beauty, all life, and all perfection!

And yet how good it is to turn away for a time from the sad and weary sight of one's own little-ness, and to lose one's self in the bright light of Thy glory!

Let me, then, O Lord, lift up my voice and join, all unworthy as I am, in the songs of the blessed, as with the accents of unfailing hope I sing from the depth of my sufferings, " Holy, holy, holy, Lord God of Sabaoth.

" Heaven and earth are full of Thy glory.

" Blessed is he that cometh in the name of the Lord."

The Canon.

O Lord, I unite my prayer not only to the ever-lasting praises which the angels sing at Thy feet, but also to those which Thy Church has re-echoed from the beginning by the mouths of her Apostles, her Martyrs, her Patriarchs, her Virgins, and all her faithful members, whether they have departed out of this world, or are still dwelling here.

Let my sacrifice be joined to the sacrifice which Thy Church unceasingly offers to Thee. From the time that Thy blood was shed for her upon the Cross, she, Thy faithful spouse, filled with a like love for Thee, has never ceased to pour out her own blood for Thy glory. Jealously desirous of making some return for Thy love, and as though inflamed with heavenly emulation, day by day she dies for Thee, and so continues, for love of Thee, to be what the Apostle calls her when he says, " We are accounted as sheep for the slaughter." *

God forbid that I should ever be shut out from the benefits of that all-prevailing sacrifice, that my oblation should be lost by being separated from the oblation which Thy Church offers to Thee. Unworthy as is my sacrifice, small as are my sufferings compared with those of Thy saints and martyrs, I yet unite the little that I suffer to the great work of their patience, so that by this august union my trials may acquire an efficacy which of themselves they could never obtain.

The Memento.

Permit me, O Lord, in virtue of that communion which unites all the souls justified by Thy love, to offer Thee my sufferings for the spiritual and temporal good of those who are dear to me, and of all whom I remember at this moment, also for the souls detained in purgatory. There is nothing in our Holy Faith more clearly established than the power of Christian suffering, united to prayer, for obtaining graces, and applying them to the souls of those we love. May my prayers and sufferings be thus availing through Thy holy grace.

* Rom. viii. 36.

The Consecration.

And now all is ready for the supreme act of sacrifice. There only remains to lay hands upon the Victim and give Him the death-blow which is necessary for every immolation.

In the holy sacrifice Thou dost constitute Thyself, Lord, truly a victim by the distinct consecration of Thy body and blood, so that the sword of the priestly word still separates symbolically that which, since Thy resurrection, is in reality inseparable; for "being risen from the dead, Christ no longer dies; death has no longer any power over Him." It is this mystery of mystical separation and death, remembrance and continuation of the dolorous separation and death on the Cross which Thou dost now propose to my soul. Now the time has come when I must die with Thee, as the Apostle understood it when he exclaimed, "Let us also go up and die with Him!"

It will not do to stop at the foot of Calvary, as so many cowardly souls do; we must *go up* and lay ourselves down upon the Cross with Thee.

O Lord Jesus, in union with that sovereign will by which at Thy command death died, and accomplished its work in Thee, I accept that same death in the spirit of sacrifice for Thy glory, for Thy love, for the salvation of those whose names are known to Thee, and for my own salvation.

I accept death in my mind by submitting to be deprived of the power of working and of all intellectual effort. I accept it by resigning myself to this cruel inaction to which illness condemns me.

I accept death in my heart, even if it is to deprive me of the enjoyment of my dearest affections, and keep me at a distance from them, or banish me from the joys which other men pursue, and condemn my life to solitude.

Above all, I accept death by renouncing the choice of my own will and by walking where Thine leads me, and by consenting to follow Thee, Lord, in that darkness of uncertainty which is the greatest of all trials. Finally, I accept death in my flesh, submitting in faith and hope to Thy supreme decree, consecrating my last hour to Thee, and breathing forth my last sigh at Thy feet beforehand in a spirit of sacrifice and as a last proof of my love.

The Communion and End of the Sacrifice.

What remains to me now, O Lord, in order to finish my immolation, and render it acceptable to Thee, but to unite it to Thine and to say with Thy Apostle, " It is no longer I who suffer; it is no longer I who die; it is no longer I who offer up myself, but it is Christ Jesus, Who suffers, Who offers Himself up, Who dies in me." O blessed communion with the holy death of Jesus; O blessed death united to His death; O death more fruitful than life itself; O death who art so transformed, that the nearer I behold thee, the more I lose sight of all that was wont to terrify me in thee! Thou art death still, and so my bodily nature is startled and confounded at thy presence, for thou art a thing contrary to nature; the hand of sin gave thee thy being, and not the hand of God. But now, clothed as thou art with the Blood of Jesus, covered with His love, adorned with His name, transfigured by the remembrance of Him, Thou art to me another name for the Cross. Lord, I am not worthy to enter into the depth of Thy mysteries; say only the word and my soul shall be healed.

Lord, teach me to unite my sacrifice to Thine, and to be one with Thee upon the Cross.

Lord, do Thou present to Thy Father the free offering of a soul which would fain die in spirit with Thee, in order to live henceforth only in Thee.

Grant, O Lord, that having thus found in the extremity of my weakness a means of glorifying Thee, I may never neglect to make due use of it.

Grant that, in the oblation and consummation of my sacrifice, I may find that treasure of strength which is to be found in every work that is done for love of Thee and to Thy glory. Let my willing submission to death, when united to and transformed by Thy death for us sinners, teach me the secret of true resurrection to the fulness of life, whether it be Thy will that I should find it in a longer continuance in this world, or in a speedy departure to that better one where there will be no more sickness, nor suffering, nor tears, nor parting, nor change, nor death; but eternal joy, peace, possession, and love. Amen.

THANKSGIVING.

The Sick Man. "Thou wilt turn, O God, and bring us to life, and Thy people shall rejoice in Thee. Shew us, O Lord, thy mercy; and grant us Thy salvation. I will hear what the Lord God will speak in me: for He will speak peace unto His people:

"And unto His saints: and unto them that are converted to the heart." *

The Comforter. Thou art wise, O my Son, in that thou doubtest not the mercy and love with which I look upon those souls who turn to Me in sincerity. I have heard thy prayers, and the voice of thine offering has come up before Me. Thou hast made generously that oblation of thyself of which the bloody sacrifice of My servant Abraham was but a figure. Recall to mind the thought of it. It will teach thee that I often prove

* Psalm lxxxiv. 7–9.

the faith of My elect ones, without requiring at
their hands the accomplishment of the sacrifices
to which I seem to call them. It is enough, in
such a case, if I implant in their souls a sincere
desire to give up everything for My glory.

Thou hast willingly accepted death at My hands;
it is well, my son ; the resolutions and the prayers
which thou hast offered to Me in this spirit of self-
oblation I have heard and blessed. Dwell no
longer on the thought of death ; the season for
such thoughts is past.

It is life, My son, which should always spring
up for thee out of meditation on death. Hear
and consider the words of My Apostle : "For you
are dead; and your life is hid with Christ in God."*
He begins by saying, " For you are dead," and
it might seem as if nothing more need be added,
for why should any words be addressed to the
dead ?   But his next words are of life—"And your
life is hid."   This same death then only hides
life, gathers it up, encloses it carefully, and so it
is nourished, strengthened in secret till the day
"when Christ shall appear, who is your life ; then
you also shall appear with Him in glory." †

Thou knowest not, My son, when this glorious
day shall be, and if I have not made it known
to thee, it is because the knowledge of it would

* Col. iii. 3.   † Col. iii. 4.

not tend to advance thy salvation. Thou needest
only to know that it will surely come, and that
it is near at hand even now.

For these words may be taken in many senses,
as often happens in My Word. Thy return to life
in the revelation of My glory may signify the
reward which awaits thy labours when this mortal
life shall be ended, and thou shalt enjoy unchanging rest in the company of My saints. It may
also mean that I have still work for thee to do
in this world, and that, after having trained thee
in the seclusion of trial, and under the shadow
of approaching death, I may, in the day when
it shall please Me, break open the grave of thy
weakness, and give thee such strength as shall
make thee unexpectedly fruitful in good works
to My glory.

My son, the soul can accomplish nothing great
in My service unless, like Me and with Me, she has
passed through death. The children of this world
cannot understand these words, and amongst the
many divine axioms which scandalize them, this
seems to them one of the hardest and most foolish.
And yet, were St. John the Baptist, St. Paul,
St. Jerome, St. Chrysostom, St. Athanasius, were
these, My saints, men according to this world?
Nay, they were dead and buried to the world, and
yet "their sound hath gone forth into all the
earth ; and their words unto the ends of the

world." * Thou seest, then, that dying to themselves, to their own desires and will, is no reason
for My sons to doubt of their future usefulness
in advancing My glory. This is, on the contrary,
the beginning of their vocation, and the mark of
My favour. When all human instrumentality fails,
let them believe that their hour draws near, for
I work only through death. Thou hast striven
to do this. So, be at rest. Drink the cup to the
dregs ; let those around thee weep over thee as
useless and incapable of any service in this world.
Bear it all in silence. Give Me yet a little time.
Let Me be the judge of thy days, and await in
unshaken confidence the hour of thy resurrection.
That hour, which will strike in time, has been fixed
from all eternity.

"SUFFICIENT FOR THE DAY IS THE EVIL ·THEREOF."

My brother, when trials come upon you, do not
weary yourself by looking into the future, and
trying to forecast the extent and the duration
of your sufferings. There is no labour on earth
more fruitless, no trouble more unavailing. Affliction comes upon us without any possibility of our
foreseeing it, and as suddenly leaves us when we
have lost all hopes of relief. This is why the wise

* Psalm xviii. 5.

man lives in a state of suspense, being neither too confident in prosperity, nor too depressed in adversity. The wisdom of this course was well known to ancient philosophy, and the poet counsels it in those beautiful lines where he says: "Stir up thy courage and thy strength in the day of adversity; and be not less wise in prosperity; but when the fair wind blows, spread not out all thy sails without reserve." But this philosophical uncertainty, inasmuch as it was only grounded on doubt and distrust, brought neither hope nor consolation to mankind. It was left for Christianity to give a foundation of Faith to uncertainty itself.

"Be not solicitous, therefore," saith the Lord Jesus, "for your Father knoweth that you have need of all these things. Be not, therefore, solicitous for to-morrow," He repeats, "for the morrow will be solicitous for itself. Sufficient for the day is the evil thereof." *

Our Lord speaks in the first place of *the Father*, next he speaks of *the Day*, and seems to imply that, in the very fact of this division of life into days, there is a source of comfort and of rest. Let us try to understand this.

I. "Your Father knoweth that you have need of all these things." What motive there is in this for rest and confidence! I do not know what is to be the end of My sickness; I can foresee

* St. Matt. vi. 31, 34.

nothing, either as to its duration or its ultimate issue. But there is One who knows; One who foresees all; One who guides my steps with unerring wisdom, whilst I walk blindly on; and this Almighty One is *my Father!* He is not less powerful than wise, nor less loving than powerful; Infinite in the threefold Unity of His wisdom, His power, and His love.

Assuredly, if we hold it true that a virtue is given to earthly parents, whereby they are enabled to see further into the future than their light-hearted, inexperienced children and to guard them in that future, through the wisdom and foresight of their love, what must we think of that Father, Who, though He is the Ruler and Creator of all the worlds, cares for each particular one of us, as if each one were His sole concern?

This all-wise and loving Father has me ever in His sight; He sees my sufferings; His knowledge is not limited to the past; He knows and foresees what the morrow has in store for me; He proportions my trials to my strength, and will never allow them to be greater than I can bear.

"But," the sufferer may argue, "why has not this omnipotent and loving Father saved me from this furnace of tribulation? You say that He can do all things, and that He loves me; if so, He might have prevented the evil that He foresaw."

And why should He have prevented it? Has it

done you any real harm? Has your soul become less pure since this trial has overtaken it? Has not the fire of suffering, on the contrary, rendered it more free from its passions and evil inclinations, and purified it, and so made it more capable of understanding the sorrows of others, more humble and compassionate—in a word, more like unto God Himself?

Believe what our Blessed Lord tells you, that your Father always watches over you, that He sees and knows your needs. Be sure that all which has come upon you hitherto has been for the good of your soul, and leave to that foreseeing and loving Father the care of the days that have yet to run. Do not wear yourself out in worrying about an unknown future, but try to live well each day as it comes, for "sufficient for the day is the evil thereof."

II. "For *the day*." It was not without a purpose that the Father of mankind divided time and life by this measure of days, and it concerns us to enter, as far as may be, into the wisdom of this divine intention, and to learn to use aright each day as it is given to us.

If the most diligent workman were shown a large building, and ordered immediately to erect a similar one, his heart would fail him, and he would give up all idea of attempting an undertaking so far beyond his strength. But if the architect, instead of exhibiting the whole plan of the building at once, only allotted him a reasonable piece of work at a time, portioning out every morning his task for the day, then the workman would set about it cheerfully, and the building would be roofed in before he had realized the magnitude of the undertaking. So it is with the building up of our own salvation. If the Divine Architect were to show to each of us human toilers the task that must be accomplished before we attain to rest, we should be overwhelmed at the sight, and give up in despair. But the wise Architect of our eternal happiness knows how to order the labour of his children. He hides from us the complete plan of the work, and only lets us see it bit by bit. He divides our task; He reckons the hours of our day; He portions out the burden according to our strength. The task which he allots us each morning is all that it concerns us to know. Let us strive to do it well, and when the evening comes, let us, like the good workman, not trouble ourselves about the labour of the morrow, but receive our day's wages, and turn homewards with a contented heart.

"Sufficient for the day is the evil thereof." Is not the portion of suffering and striving which the Divine Master has allotted to you to-day sufficient? Why do you keep looking out for the burden which will only come to-morrow? Thank God for having hidden it from you; thank Him for having

ordered the succession of times and seasons, so as
to give rest to a nature so frail and so incapable of
unbroken effort.

A day will come when this succession of seasons
will cease. The last sun of the world will set, to
be followed by the endless dawn of the eternal day.
Then we shall see at one glance the amount of
work which, by the help of God, and His merciful
division of our labours, we have been able to
accomplish during life. I cannot but think that the
elect will then be surprised at the extent of their
own work, and that, whilst ascribing to God alone
all the glory thereof, they will nevertheless wonder
that it should have been achieved by them. Just
as when the poor artisan, after having toiled through
the long summer days, stands amidst the crowd
before the majestic building which his hands have
helped to raise, and hears them praising its magnifi-
cence and its strength, we can fancy him wondering
whether he can really have had a share in carrying
out so grand an edifice, and feeling genuine admiration for the architect, who, with short-lived men for
his instruments, has raised a monument that will
endure throughout the ages. How much more
shall we exult in the blessed revelation of our
earthly labours when the great day of reward shall
come ! Dazzled by the glories and beauties of that
living Jerusalem, which, under God's grace, our
strivings and sufferings in this world have helped

K

to build, we shall exclaim wonderingly to the angels, " How can the endeavours of a few passing years have sufficed to create such a glorious work!" And their voices will answer, " Sufficient for the day is the evil thereof."

"WE ARE UNPROFITABLE SERVANTS."

" We are unprofitable servants." These are assuredly true words, in that they ascribe all glory to God alone ; and humble words, since they abase us in His sight, and remind us that we are never necessary to the accomplishment of His designs. But, in order that they may not lose their true meaning, we must take care to understand them rightly, and to use them in the sense in which our Blessed Saviour pronounced them. For we may use them in a true spirit of humility, after having accomplished the most heroic labours ; or, in a spirit of discouragement and indolence, after yielding without a struggle to our slothful inclinations, and then seeking an excuse for this self-indulgence in expressions of cowardice and false humility.

The state of languor to which a lingering illness reduces us predisposes us to faint-heartedness, and unless we make vigorous efforts to shake off this torpor, we shall end by giving way to it altogether, to the great prejudice of the body as well as of the soul ; for the body is weakened by mental weakness, and thereby rendered less fit to resist the attacks of sickness. When illness is upon us, or has left behind it a state of chronic exhaustion, we are apt to become absorbed in the consideration of our own sufferings. We listen eagerly to well-meant but mistaken advice on this subject, and give up reading and everything else which would serve to divert our minds, but which at the same time requires some exertion. The soul sinks, so to speak, with the body, and makes no attempt at reaction towards life. Religion itself has no longer power to lift up the soul thus borne down to earth ; nay, the poor soul contrives to justify its own weakness, by answering to every appeal to its prostrate energy, "We are unprofitable servants."

But all have not an equal right to use these words, and none less so than they who give themselves up too easily to self-indulgence. Our Blessed Lord says, "When you shall have done all things that are commanded you, say, "We are unprofit-able servants ; we have done that which we ought to do." * So we see that this passage, far from assuming the inactivity of the servant, presupposes, on the contrary, courage, diligence, faithful service, crowned by true humility.

But this humility must be preceded by deeds, not mere words ; self-devotion and effort are needful to give it efficacy. It is the firm resolve to do

* St. Luke xvii. 10.

our duties, and perseverance in their fulfilment, which gives a soul the right to humble itself with honour before Almighty God, and to say to Him, "We are unprofitable servants." Separated from deeds, these words become a mere truism, and confession of cowardice. In order to come with sincerity from the mouth of a Christian, they must be accompanied by active service. But what can the active work of a sick man be?

The answer to this will, of course, depend on the nature of his illness. It is obvious that the duties of an invalid must vary according as his sickness either deprives him altogether of his powers of mind and body, or leaves him in command of them, but weakened and impaired. We will consider the first of these cases, and see if even this will not allow of a very noble kind of activity. The whole Stoic philosophy was, so to speak, contained in one word, the stern energy of which can hardly be misunderstood, " *Sustine*"—endure !

This proud watchword, uttered by the Stoics with all the insolence of pagan pride, becomes noble and salutary on the lips of a Christian, when its arrogance is tempered by the humility of the Gospel.

Sustine—endure ! Young soldier of Christ, stricken by the cruel hand of disease, dry those tears that are wrung from you by longings for an active life. *Sustine !* God, your Master and your

Friend, sees your longings, reckons up your struggles, and employs to the glory of His name and the coming of His kingdom every hard-won victory of your patience. When, after a weary day, spent in striving to conquer your own will, you commend your soul at night into the hands of God, take courage, for you have earned the right to repeat with sincerity those words of the faithful labourer, "*Lord, we are unprofitable servants ; we have done that which we ought to do.*"

Sustine ! Endure, above all, O soul consecrated to God, my brother in the priesthood, withheld by sickness from those labours for which you gave up all worldly callings, and afflicted because you may no longer share the Church's toils and weariness. When in the evening you turn your thoughts to your flock, and sigh as you remember that all day long you have been unable to leave your bed in order to feed your people with the Word of God, take courage ! God sees the desires of the heart ; He accepts them, He blesses them, and makes them fruitful for the good of souls. You, too, have laboured faithfully, and you may fearlessly make these words your own, "*We are unprofitable servants.*"

Sustine ! Endure, Christian soul, whoever you may be, whose strength is brought low by weakness, and whose generous desires for the glory of God seem doomed never to be of any use to the

holy cause you are so anxious to serve. Call faith
to your aid, and do not fancy yourself forsaken
because God does not at this moment accept from
you any visible labour. Say to yourself again and
again that God does not need our restless agitation,
and that the ceaseless activity of Martha conduces
less to his glory than the silent contemplation of
Mary.

Know, moreover, that *to suffer is to do;* and that
the hidden work of silent resignation in suffering
and helplessness raises the soul to the rank of
those faithful servants who, whilst unprofitable in
their own eyes, are by patience and humility
helping to complete the immortal work of Jesus
Christ.

COURAGE AND WORK.

The Sick Man. My brother, I am not of the
number of those of whom you speak—those who
are laid low by serious illness, or by constant
suffering. My health is not destroyed, only
weakened ; I do not sink under my sickness, but
I falter under it as a burden too heavy for my
daily strength. I cannot reckon on my strength
from one hour to another, or feel sure of being able
to finish anything that I begin.

This weakness and uncertainty discourage me
from working at all. What can I do with such

unstable and failing powers ?   It is only by regular
and persevering effort that the human mind can
accomplish any adequate result.   What can I
attempt amidst the continually recurring inter-
ruptions of illness ?   What can I undertake when
I am so constantly obliged to go from one place
to another ?   It seems better to wait for the return
of health before beginning anything.   When I
shall have regained my bodily strength, and can
count on my powers, then I will begin something
worthy of God's glory, and of the warmth of my
zeal for His service.

The Friend.   My brother, you are labouring
under a delusion.   What you look upon as weakness of body, is much more in reality—cowardice
of soul.   Remember, that a man's work on earth
is not measured by the amount of physical strength,
but of will and energy which he puts into it.   Look
at the armies of this world, and see how they carry
on their work of warfare.   Do you suppose that
victory is always on the side of the largest and
strongest army ?   All history, whether sacred or
profane, tells us, on the contrary, that stout hearts,
not numbers, gain the day.   Courage is the real
strength of an army, and a determination to
conquer is the surest pledge of conquest.   And this
truth applies equally to those bloodless struggles
that are fought out in the heart of every individual
life.   Work is always a struggle, in which nothing

but a strong will ensures the victory, and this victory is achieved at the cost of self-sacrifice.

Self-sacrifice is the one fruitful source of action in life ; we must be able to give up our own wills, to forget ourselves, to die to self, or else we shall never be fit to bear the fatigue and strain which every great undertaking involves, or to overcome the disgust which nature feels for labour.

If we wait to undertake any work till we feel quite up to it, and feeling in perfect health, the chances are we are condemning ourselves to a thoroughly useless and idle life. Few of us are ever absolutely free from bodily suffering of some sort, and those most to be envied are they who can forget their ailments, and work on in spite of them. What personal exertions will not a man of business make for the advancement of his fortune, even when it is already a large one ? He will sit up far into the night, and rise early after a few short hours' sleep, and contrive to be here, there, and everywhere, never giving a thought to his own fatigue. And this because his body is swayed by his mind, and forced to adapt itself to the will and exigencies of its master. Every ruling passion, whether it be the love of money, or of science, or of pleasure, gives the mind this power over the body.

There is one ruling passion which ought to possess every Christian soul ; this is the desire to labour incessantly for the coming of God's kingdom, and the triumph of His justice. Happy are those souls who are possessed with this passion to the exclusion of every other, and to whom it stands in lieu of every pleasure and pursuit, of fame, of science, nay, even of happiness! Such souls become all will in the service of God, all courage and self-devotion. They do not grumble about their fatigues, or the probability of their being worn out by their labours; on the contrary, they are ready to "lose their life for the Gospel's sake." And they do in truth lose that selfish and faint-hearted life which degrades and weakens so many souls, and, in its stead, they find true life, according to the Saviour's promise. A noble, large-hearted life, fruitful in good works, giving and receiving blessings, and reaping even in this world a plentiful reward in the greatness of its labours, and the depths of its joys.

The joys of work! Of Christian work, achieved in self-denial for God alone, done under His eye, and in union with Him, and free from all low ambitions, or selfish aims. What unspeakable comfort does such work bring with it! Work such as this, even when it is accomplished under great difficulties, under physical weakness and the repugnance and shrinking of nature, becomes in the end a physical remedy, inasmuch as it carries us for the time being over fatigue and depression.

" There is no sorrow," says Montesquieu, "to which
an hour's study will not bring relief."

See, Christian soul, what a holy and important
matter work really is, and do not too easily give
it up because of bodily infirmities.   Remember
that, since the beginning of the warfare between
the flesh and the spirit, the perfect equilibrium of
these two powers is rarely to be met with, and that
if the flesh is not a little weaker than the spirit,
this would soon lead to its tyrannizing over its
rival.   More men are hindered from work by the
dead weight of the flesh, than by its sufferings.
Keep constantly before your eyes the examples of
the many saints and great men who accomplished
great undertakings in spite of bodily weakness and
painful maladies.   The Roman breviary says of
St. Gregory the Great, "We cannot but admire
all that he said, did, wrote, and decreed, oppressed
as he was by constant infirmities and lingering
sickness."   We must not, however, imagine that,
even with this great man, nature had not her hours
of triumph, when the human will flagged and
threatened to sink under the strain, perpetually
thwarted as it was in its effort to resist and to
work on in spite of the prostration and suffering
of the body.

In several of his writings, in his commentary on
Ezechiel, in some of his homilies, and in many of
his letters, he bitterly deplores the hindrance his

ill-health is to him in the exercise of his ministry.
" For nearly two years," he writes to Eulogius, " I
have been confined to my room by sickness, which
causes me such acute pain, that sometimes I have
not strength to bear it. Yet pain is not the greatest
of my trials. ¡ This illness has reduced me to such
a state that I am incapable of performing any
ecclesiastical function ; this is my greatest grief.
Alas ! I can never leave my sick-bed, nor approach
the holy altar ; I am, as it were, suspended from
celebrating the Sacred Mysteries. Think what an
unceasing martyrdom this state must be to one
who only longs for health that he may be able to
fulfil his duty and do his work."

These are the lamentations of human nature.
But, if we compare them with what we read in
history of the life of St. Gregory, we find this great
man ruling the affairs of the world from his sick-
bed ; enriching the Catholic liturgy ; reforming the
morals of the clergy ; composing his famous
pastoral rule ; organizing missions in every direction ; treating with the Lombards and converting
them to the faith ; mediating between them and
the Exarchs of the Greek empire ; conducting
political matters with unflinching firmness in a time
of the greatest difficulty ; watching and directing
all that takes place in distant regions ; founding
the great Anglo-Saxon mission, supporting, watching over, and guiding it ; and all this from that

sick-bed, the scene of the continual pain and suffering of which he complains so sadly. If we consider this glorious spectacle of a soul doing battle with the body, and constantly coming off victorious, it will teach us more forcibly than any exhortations, that we must fight against the weakness and infirmity of our body, and that we may come to fulfil the work which is given us to do, in spite of very great suffering and exhaustion.

Remember the answer of a generous soul when she was advised to give herself some rest—" Let us work now, we shall have all eternity to rest."

WE OUGHT TO LOVE OUR ROOM.

The author of the " Imitation of Christ " says : " The cell continually dwelt in groweth sweet ; but ill guarded, it begetteth weariness. If, in the beginning of thy religious life, thou dwell in it and keep it well, it will be to thee afterwards as a dear friend and most delightful solace."* This beautiful maxim, which might seem at first sight to be written only for monks, on coming to be examined bears a close application to all Christian souls. It is true for all alike, that our taste for the interior life depends very much on first habits, and that we gain or lose this taste according as we make a practice of giving some time daily to

* Imit. book i. ch. xx.

spiritual reading and meditation, or give ourselves up entirely to the busy triflings of this world.

But this sentence of the "Imitation" contains especial comfort for sick people, for it reminds them that they may find an unexpected source of happiness in what, at first sight, seemed calculated only to cause them weariness and depression.

Let us suppose that the doctor has just left you, after examining into the state of your health, and drawing his conclusions as to the motives for hope or fear which it presents. He has told you that, as far as he can see, you will be obliged to keep your room for some time. He has delivered this sentence, and gone away, and you are now alone in your sick-room.

How are you going to adapt yourself to this room which God has kindly provided for you as a place of refuge in the hour of your weakness? In what spirit are you going to take possession of it? Is it to be in a cheerful or a sullen temper? Depend upon it, this is a matter of no small importance. Instead of sitting down gloomily, and looking round you with fretfulness and vexation; instead of flattening your face against the window-pane, and thinking impatiently of the pleasure it would be to escape from your room, take my advice and make friends with it. It will be kind to you, if you look kindly on it; and after all you are more dependent on your room than it on you.

Take possession of it, then, in a gentle and kindly frame of mind; stifle at once all bitter repinings; the first beginnings in this case are very important. " Shut thy door upon thee, and call unto thee Jesus, thy Beloved." * Tell this faithful Friend that the prospect of a longer and closer communion with Him has no terrors for you, and that, in order to profit by it more fully, you will accept without murmuring all the privations which this retreat will inflict upon your human nature. It will be well for you to have this chamber, which you must inhabit for so long a time, filled with the adorable presence of your Divine Friend. Beg Him to be constantly with you; accept gladly the conditions on which He agrees to come to you. Be willing to bear all the trials He lays upon you; do not refuse anything. Accept it all graciously.

And now, look round your room again; do you not find that everything seems different? What is there, after all, so gloomy and terrible about this quiet spot in which you are going to live? It knows you intimately, and if you have not as yet learned to appreciate the charm of its solitary intercourse, the fault lies not in it, but in yourself. Treat it, then, as you would a person whose good graces you wished to win. Adorn it a little, and be careful to have it kept in good order. Neatness in your room is, so to speak, an extension of neatness in

* Imit. book i. ch. xx.

your person, and both are especially necessary to
the sick. If your chamber is well ordered, it will
be more pleasing to you ; if it is dark, this will
make it seem lighter ; if poor, it will have that
which can adorn poverty itself. For my own part,
I don't think I could ever love a magnificent apartment, luxuriously fitted up, and furnished with all
kind of vanities. It would be hardly possible to
find intimate companionship in such a room, made
for the crowd, suitable enough for noisy festivities,
but forlorn and dull in solitude. Thus one may be
master of a palace, and still not have what can be
called one's *own room*. And so, all that I have
been saying may apply to the poorest and simplest
apartment.

Let your little cell be ever so plain, it will
probably contain some things of which poverty
need not deprive the poorest. These things are
familiar objects, but it is probably a long time
since you condescended to look at them. Look at
them now. Have a little more consideration for
them, and remember that they are not without
their special value and importance. If you doubt
this, God grant that it may never be brought home
to you by experiencing the misery engendered by
the want of them in a strange place. A clever
man, who was confined for some time to his room,
once wrote a book of travels, and called it "A
Journey round my Room." This would be a

capital journey for an invalid to make. Let me persuade you to undertake it cheerfully, and with good will, and you will be surprised at the wonderful discoveries you will make during the expedition. Men who have been twice round the world, may have found out less that is worthy of note than a poor recluse may meet with in his journey round his own room.

All depends upon your manner of travelling ; we find little more on a journey than we carry with us, and you may take with you on this one an amount of patience, of memories, of good desires, of hope and energy, that will carry you, almost without your being aware of it, to heights whence there will suddenly spread out before your astonished gaze the two objects best worth knowing in the whole universe—God and your soul.

Cheer up, then, and set out on your travels. Two or three months seem interminable in prospect, but they will be over before you have well started on the great journey. Explore the ever-new region of meditation on spiritual things. At every turn in these paths new scenes will open before you, and you will find in them a remedy for the constant longing after change which is likely to beset you. Nothing is so tormenting to the poor invalid as this same demon of change. The whole earth presents but little variety in comparison with the soul and the spiritual kingdom, and it is in this

spiritual kingdom that we must endeavour to make
unceasing advances; here alone we may safely
give way to insatiable longings and boundless
wishes. For the whole world is smaller than the
heart of man, and nothing is great but God. And
God is most easily to be found in that quiet and
seclusion of which the author of the "Imitation"
speaks so lovingly. My brother, you have your
quiet cell, you have your books to converse with,
your pictures to amuse you, your letters and papers
to remind you gently of the past, your Crucifix to
reassure you as to the future, and if a man be truly
wise, less even than all this will suffice to make
him happy. Learn, then, to love your room.

ANXIETY.

The Sick Man. Lord, it is neither the greatness
nor the duration of my sufferings that now
oppresses me; it is rather the uncertainty as
regards the issue of my sickness, and the over-
whelming anxiety which this causes me. All my
future life is shrouded in doubt; I no longer dare
to look forward, nor can I venture to lay any plans
of the most trifling kind. I have consulted
physicians of skill and experience, but none of
them will hazard an opinion as to the duration, or
final issue of my illness; their silence disquiets
me; and I almost regret the false hopes with

which they have hitherto buoyed me up. My
friends and relations, seeing how anxious I am,
think to allay my anxiety by constant assurance
of a speedy cure. I do not contradict them ; I
listen to what they tell me, and even try to comfort
them by pretending to believe all they say. But,
when I am alone, I break down under the double
burden of their and my own anxiety.

Lord, when will the gloom of this suspense be
illuminated by a ray of light? I do not ask to
know if I shall recover, I ask only to know what
is to happen to me. I long to raise the thick veil
which throws its shadow over my life. Lord, hear
and answer my prayer!

The Comforter. My son, thou didst offer thyself
to Me ; be not astonished, therefore, to find that
I have accepted thy offering, and permitted the
enemy to try the strength of thy love.

" Son, when thou comest to the service of God,
prepare thy soul for temptation.

" Humble thy heart and endure, and make not
haste in the time of clouds.

" Wait on God with patience : join thyself to
God, and endure, that thy life may be increased in
the latter end.

" Take all that shall be brought upon thee : and
in thy sorrow endure, and in thy humiliation keep
patience.

" For gold and silver are tried in the fire, but
acceptable men in the furnace of humiliation.

"Believe God, and He will recover thee: and direct thy way, and trust in Him.

"Ye that fear the Lord, wait for His mercy: and go not aside from Him, lest ye fall.

"Ye that fear the Lord, believe Him: and your reward shall not be void.

"Ye that fear the Lord, hope in Him: and mercy shall come to you for your delight.

"Ye that fear the Lord, love Him and your hearts shall be enlightened.

"My children, behold the generations of men: and know ye that no one hath hoped in the Lord, and hath been confounded.

"For who hath continued in His commandment, and hath been forsaken? or who hath called Him, and He despised him?

"For God is compassionate and merciful, and will forgive sins in the day of tribulation: and He is a protector to all who seek Him in truth." *

Once again, My son, suffer not the long and uncertain continuance of thy sickness to sadden or tempt thee. Remember how many protestations of trust and resignation thou hast made at My feet. Wouldst thou rather that, instead of taking thee at thy word, I had treated thee as one of those doubtful friends whose promises of fidelity are not to be relied upon?

How many times hast thou said before Mine

* Eccles. ii. 1-13.

altar, "Lord, into Thy hands I commend my spirit ; Lord, I close mine eyes, and trust only in Thee. Do Thou lead me, guide me, and dispose of me without any will of my own. I accept whatever Thou willest ; I bow to whatever Thou ordainest ; I give myself up wholly to Thee."

Dost thou not know, My child, that words like these are not to be lightly uttered, and that I hold all such generous expressions as binding on the soul ?

What soldiers are chosen for the post of honour, where danger lies ? Is it not they who have volunteered for such duties over and over again, and who have asked as a favour to be placed in the front of the battle ? Thou hast done this, and I have taken thee at thy word.

Do not give way, then ; be not discouraged at the assaults of the enemy ; endure, and await My help. If I delay for a while, be sure that it is only the better to secure thy victory, and the better to show forth the courage of those who serve Me.

Why dost thou desire to know the future, and the final issue of thy sufferings ? If thou wert assured that they must end in death, would there not be danger that in thy present state of weakness thou wouldst lose thy peace of mind ? And if, on the other hand, thou wert assured of thy speedy recovery, where would be the merit of thy self-oblation and thy patient trust in Me ? Be assured, then, that I do all for the salvation of thy soul, and continue faithful, even in the midst of complete uncertainty.

Hast thou not read in the history of My passion, how, after being taken in the garden, I was led to the high priest's house, and how, during the night that followed, "they blindfolded Me," and "smote My face? And they asked Me, saying, Prophesy, who is it that struck Thee?"* Think of Me in this state of cruel agony, and remember that I bore it all in order to strengthen and sustain thee in the depth of thy anxiety and suspense, blindfolded and bound as thou art in the darkness of prolonged suffering. I bore it all to teach thee that the glorious dawn of the Resurrection is nearer than thou thinkest to the darkest hour of sorrow.

The Sick Man. Lord, I adore Thee, beaten with rods by the impious soldiers, blindfolded and silent before the blasphemous mockings of Thy tormentors, and answering nothing to those who cried, "Prophesy, who is it that struck Thee?" I, too, am blinded by the darkness of suffering which overshadows me; I am full of uncertainty, and unable to give any answer to the questionings of others, or to those of my own anxiety. I unite my darkness to Thy patient blindness, my silence to Thy silence, and so, in faith and hope, I wait upon Thine adorable will.

* St. Luke xxii. 64.

STRENGTH PERFECTED IN WEAKNESS.

It was winter. The night was dark and cold, as a man and a woman wended their way along one of the roads of Judea. They were drawing near Bethlehem. The appearance of the lonely way-farers would have excited a movement of compassion or of contempt in the mind of a passer-by, accordingly as he chanced to be of a kindly or a heartless disposition. They were evidently poor to wretchedness. The woman seemed very weary. She stopped from time to time to take rest, and then calling God to her aid, went on. Nothing, to all human appearance, could be less likely to influence the destinies of the world than these two humble travellers. And yet this hour of their uttermost fatigue and exhaustion was the crowning hour of ages; the hour desired by the patriarchs, the hour which all creation had been awaiting in throes of unspeakable expectation. Heaven itself was attentive, and when at midnight this obscure woman brought forth her firstborn Son, the angelic choirs sang out, " Glory to God on earth."

Why, then, will you measure the greatness of God's designs on you by your own weakness? When will you learn and believe that God wills to advance His glory by means of your nothingness? When will you understand that He has

chosen the weak things of the world to confound
the things which are mighty?

O you, who feel your strength giving way, and
who, halting on life's road, are asking sorrowfully
why God has brought you to such extremities, lift
up your head, and hope. What is mortal "is sown
in" man's "weakness," to be raised in the "power"
of God; "it is sown in corruption" to be "raised
in incorruption;" "it is sown in dishonour" to be
"raised in glory." *

Think of the elect of God, whom He has chosen
to accomplish His greatest works, whom He has
selected above all others to advance His glory.
They have been weak in the eyes of the world, but
their very weakness has been a source of strength
to them, so that in the hour of conflict they have
been suddenly transformed into leaders of the
people. Who "recovered strength from weakness,
became valiant in war." †

*Convaluerunt de infirmitate, fortes facti sunt in
bello !*

If you were strong with the strength of this
world, you might more reasonably fear to be over-
looked by God, and considered in some sort unfitted
for His work; for He seldom makes use of the
mighty ones of the earth; they are too stubborn
and proud to be flexible instruments in His hands,
and too prone to seek their own advantage rather

* 1 Cor. xv. 42, 43. † Heb. xi. 34.

than His glory. But you have been broken by suffering, and being thus taught to know your own weakness, you have gained thereby a special fitness for God's service.

The Apostle was well aware of this, and rejoiced in the thought with holy exaltation: "If I must needs glory, I will glory of the things which concern my infirmity." * Again, "Gladly therefore will I glory in my infirmities, that the power of Christ may dwell in me."† And lastly, "For which cause I please myself in my infirmities, in reproaches, in necessities, in persecutions, in distresses for Christ; for when I am weak, then am I powerful."‡

Strange words, that sound like a paradox. And verily it is a sublime paradox, which places strength in weakness, because the humble weakness of the servant calls forth the all-powerful aid of the Master; and thus that strength, which can do all things, is born and perfected in want of strength. "Strength is made perfect in weakness."

Leave, then, to the worldly man the pride of his vain strength; be not troubled, O Christian, if he despise you for your weakness, for the poverty of your intellect, for your want of fortune, of bodily health, of influence. You are weak, it is true, but with the help of God you will be able to attack the giant, "who shall not be saved by his own great

* 2 Cor. xi. 30.   † 2 Cor. xii. 9.   ‡ 2 Cor. xii. 10.

strength," * and those who look on will ask how it has come to pass, that almost before the struggle has begun, Goliath has fallen under the despised arm of David. You yourself will be astonished at your own victories, and, since the knowledge of your own weakness will keep you from taking the credit of them to yourself, you will ascribe the glory where alone it is due—to the Lord God Almighty, Who is the corner-stone and strength of all who trust in Him.

The Physician.

" Honour the physician for the need thou hast of him : for the Most High hath created him.

"For all healing is from God, and He shall receive gifts of the king.

" The skill of the physician shall lift up his head, and in the sight of great men he shall be praised.

" The Most High hath created medicines out of the earth, and a wise man will not abhor them.

" Was not bitter water made sweet with wood ?

" The virtue of these things is come to the knowledge of men, and the Most High hath given knowledge to men, that he may be honoured in his wonders.

" By these he shall cure and shall allay their pains, and of these the apothecary shall make

---

* Psalm xxxii. 16.

sweet confections, and shall make up ointments of health, and of his works there shall be no end.

"For the peace of God is over all the face of the earth.

"My son, in thy sickness neglect not thyself, but pray to the Lord, and He shall heal thee.

"Turn away from sin, and order thy hands aright, and cleanse thy heart from all offence.

"Give a sweet savour, and a memorial of fine flour, and make a fat-offering, and then give place to the physician.

"For the Lord created him: and let him not depart from thee, for his works are necessary.

"For there is a time when thou must fall into their hands:

"And they shall beseech the Lord, that He would prosper what they give for ease and remedy, for their conversation." *

In this passage Holy Scripture teaches the sick man the true relation in which he should stand towards his physician; he must trust, but not blindly, and be grateful first to God, and then to the physician.

Most people are either utterly incredulous, or absolutely superstitious with regard to medical men. People in health are apt to scoff at them; people who have never known suffering speak contemptuously of them; there are, in fact, *esprits*

* Eccles. xxxviii. 1–14.

forts in medicine as well as in religion. And, on the other hand, in medicine as well as in religion, there is a narrow-minded credulity which is a kind of superstition. We must be careful not to fall into either of these extremes, for both are contrary to reason and common sense. Do not indulge in those silly, ignorant jokes with which some people greet the very name of a doctor. They are unworthy of a man or woman of sense. Next to the science of the soul, there is no nobler science than that which treats of the human frame, and he who possesses it holds a great power over other men.

Have you ever assisted at one of these surgical operations in which some vital organ is dealt with? When the knife has cut into the quivering flesh, and the life-blood of the patient flows from the wound, the surgeon alone remains calm and self-possessed, even while holding life and death in his hands. Every one else is agitated, overcome perhaps; but he works on, absorbed in his work, in his responsibility, in the tremendous stakes that hang on the steadiness of his hand, the unwavering glance of his eye.

I can think of no spectacle to be compared to this for interest and grandeur; it reminds us of the work of God Himself. If you can turn away from such a sight without feeling profound reverence for the man who has thus renewed the life of his brother man, I pity you ; and you will certainly not enter into what I am now going to write.

"*Honour the physician.*" Honour him for his science, honour him for the beneficent vocation which he has received from God, honour him for his self-devotion, for the power he has of affording us relief, and often of curing us altogether. But honour him as a man, whose power is limited ; and demand of him no more than he is able to perform, and do not look for impossibilities at his hands.

There are some people, even religious people, who dishonour God by unreasonable expectations, continually asking for things which it would be contrary to His wisdom to grant. In order to content them, the plan of Divine Providence should be reversed, and the course of God's eternal laws interrupted almost daily as their fancies might suggest. These presumptuous demands cannot be otherwise than displeasing to Almighty God ; they are the result of ignorance and of superstition, which is a disease of the soul and very dangerous to true religion. And, as I said just now, superstition is not confined to religion alone. Nothing is more common than to see people pass, in their estimate of the medical profession, from contemptuous scepticism to blind, fanatical confidence ; and the same man who, in rude health a little while ago, ridiculed all doctors as ignorant quacks,

now that he is ill pins his faith on one of the
number as if he were a demi-god, and expects him
to perform impossibilities; he expects him to
arrest the course of a fatal disease and bring back
a person from the very jaws of death, and when the
medical man fails to do this, he is an impostor or
a fool. All this is irrational and absurd. It is
not given to man to emulate the power of God.
When his friends and pupils congratulated Ambrose
Paré on the marvellous cures that he performed,
the great physician invariably replied, "I prescribed
for him, but God cured him."

Remember, moreover, that it is not every
physician who deserves the confidence which Scripture bids us place in him. Père Gratry has written:
"Many doctors think they have studied man,
while in reality they have only been studying the
animal part of him."

Man is not an animal. "Man," says Leibnitz,
"is a compound of time and eternity." It is by
his soul that he lives through eternity, for eternity
is the *time* of the soul, as infinity is its resting-
place. The soul, then, is the most important part
of man. What, then, are we to think of those
who, in their study of mankind, take no account
of the soul? It enters, nevertheless, into all the
phenomena of the physical life, and plays an important and inseparable part in the bodily life of
man—in his pleasures, his infirmities, his sufferings,

his diseases. The medical man who does not believe in the soul, and who does not take into account its co-operation in the life and death of the body, is not a counsellor to be trusted. He may know you twenty years, but if he does not believe in your soul, he does not know you really.

Remember this when you are placing yourself in his hands. The physician to whom you entrust the cure of your health will inevitably have some influence, direct or indirect, upon your spiritual life ; it becomes therefore of consequence, to your soul as well as your body, to discriminate well before selecting him.

REMEDIES.

God is everywhere.

This is one of those very simple, but, at the same time, very deep truths in which we all believe ; but vaguely and without realizing it.

God is everywhere.

St. Paul tells us that He is " not far from every one of us : for in Him we live, and move, and are." *

If it be true that God is everywhere, He must needs be in the ray of wisdom which illuminates your mind, as well as in the ray of sunshine which enlightens your bodily eyes ; He is present in the

* Acts xvii. 27, 28.

truth which feeds your understanding, as well as in the food which nourishes your body ; He is in the sacrament which sanctifies your soul, as well as in the medicine which restores your physical health. ˙ Have you ever quite realized this ?

When, in time of sickness, some healing remedy has been prescribed for you, and you have found in some natural substance ease, strength, and renewed life, have you adored God under the veil of His creature ? Oh ! the blindness of mankind, for ever making use of created things, without even dreaming that there is anything in them beyond their own natural properties. Men are surrounded on all sides by God, and yet they perceive Him not.

This outward and material nature grows in greatness and in light when we look upon it ; not merely in itself, but as the workmanship and instrument of God. Nature, in her beneficent resources, is not merely the fortunate coincidence of salutary powers happily combined ; she is the instrument of God's providence, the expression of His love.

St. Thomas Aquinas says : " God acts in every agent. . . . God is the essential cause of action in every agent. He is the first and principal agent of all action, so that He works in each particular action of His creatures ; and if it be true that the first cause is greater than the second cause, we must own that God acts more powerfully than His creature in each particular action."

Theology teaches us that two distinct graces, or virtues, are to be found in every sacrament of the Catholic Church. A common grace which is, so to speak, the foundation of the sacrament; this we call "sanctifying grace;" and a special and particular virtue, which is varied according to the special object of the sacrament, and is called "sacramental grace." And what do we mean by grace, but the active Presence of Incarnate God in the supernatural order? When we speak, then, of sanctifying, or of sacramental grace, we mean the presence of God working supernaturally, whether in a general or a special manner. Now, so far as it is lawful to assimilate and compare the mysteries of the two orders of grace and of nature, we may see a certain likeness in the way in which Almighty God works in both. In nature, as well as in grace, God works in two ways: first, in one uniform manner, in which He is the first cause of the existence of each substance; and secondly, in a special and particular manner, by which He gives to each substance its own proper virtue. God, then, not only originates and continues in existence the healing water to which you have recourse for the cure of your malady; He also works in it in an especial manner, applying the effects of the waters to your particular use, making them beneficial in your case, whilst they have no effect in the case of others. It is not only allowable, but wise and

right, to ask God to increase the efficacy of a
remedy, to bless it, to apply it more especially to
your particular case. In this there is neither
narrowness of mind nor superstitious practice, but
it all rests on reasonable foundation.

OBEDIENCE.

" I beseech you, therefore, brethren, by the mercy
of God, that you present your bodies a living
sacrifice, holy, pleasing unto God, your reasonable
service." *

These words of the Apostle may be applied to
the case of sick people, for to them, above all, this
exhortation to " reasonable service" comes with
especial fitness.

" Do what is right," says St. Anselm, "but in
such sort that you may always be able to give a
reason for it."

"Let your obedience be reasonable," says St.
Basil ; "that is to say, do God's will intelligently,
circumspectly, discreetly, and advisedly. Follow
the guidance of reason in your obedience, instead
of being led away by excited feelings."

"Reason," says St. Bernard, "is the regulator
and guide of all virtues, affections, and morals.
Reason brings order to bear upon well-doing, and
with order come proportion, beauty, and constancy.

* Rom. xii. 1.

Take away reason, and virtue itself will change into vice."

All this is intended by the holy Fathers to apply to the obedience of the Christian to God ; and if obedience of this sort must be reasonable, what shall we say of that which we owe to man ? What do we understand by reasonable obedience?

There is an unreasonable obedience contrary to duty and common sense ; it is that sort of super-stition, that blind reliance, which leads us to expect more from a man than he can possibly perform. There are invalids who sum up every-thing in the oracular remark, "My medical man has said so and so." Now, when the medical man instead of being an upright, conscientious, en-lightened man, happens to be a worldly, interested, and irreligious man, we may imagine the conse-quences of this blind faith in him. He will say that the church is too cold, and his patients will at once give up all idea of going ; he will say that reading is too fatiguing, and they will give up reading ; he will insinuate that God's commands are unreason-able, and they will disobey God at his suggestion.

I imagine, however, that your difficulties are more likely to lie in another direction. The Apostle tells us that "obedience is right, and a reasonable service." Now, what circumstances render the obedience of the sick man to his physician reason-able, nay, even a duty which is agreeable to God ?

In the first place, the confidence you place in your physician will make your obedience reasonable. A man whose goodness and skill are known to you, and whose character you respect, has a right to be obeyed ; such a man will take your soul into account, because he has a care for his own ; he will not lightly sacrifice your spiritual welfare to the supposed interests of your body. The aim of such a physician in prescribing for you will be to restore you to health, in order that you may be able to do your duties and fulfil your vocation in life.

Now, amongst all the motives which may tend to make your obedience reasonable, none has more weight than this wish to be enabled to resume your duties and your divine vocation.

This vocation embraces both body and soul. Every soul which comes into this world has some particular design of God to fulfil, some part of the divine programme to execute. This it is which constitutes a " vocation ; " and the body of which it takes possession on entering the world is the instrument intended to aid it in carrying out the divine plan. The special duties of the body, corresponding as they do to the higher vocation of the soul, are certainly the noblest portion of physical life. A soul does not become the possessor of its allotted body for the mere purpose of the ordinary and commonplace uses to which this body may be turned ; there is a special use to be made of it, agreeably to the vocation which the soul has received from God. Thus the military man will inure his body to fatigue, and the use of arms ; the priest will cultivate self-devotion, and purity of the senses as well as of the soul ; the artist will labour to acquire steadiness and precision of eye and hand; the orator to master emphatic tones and noble language ; the physician will strive after quickness of perception ; the student will pursue learning in lengthened vigils by the midnight lamp. Thus the chief use of the body is to share in the vocation and destiny of the soul. If, therefore, you find that through sickness your body is likely to become un-fitted for the service of God, and the fulfilment of its vocation, it is a duty you owe to God to use every lawful means to regain bodily strength.

But if it should happen that the prescriptions of your medical man thwart and hinder the interests of your vocation, instead of advancing them, then it may be necessary to resist, or, at any rate, to consider.

Remember that you are not sent into this world to live as long as possible at any cost, but to do God's work in it, even though that work should require great and continued self-denial.

St. Augustine complains frequently in his writings of sufferings from violent headaches. We may reasonably suspect that his medical man often advised him to give up work, and if so we may be sure the saint thanked the learned doctor, and quietly continued his vigils. One day, when that saint-like soul, Sœur Rosalie, was very ill, and had been forbidden by the doctor to go out to visit the poor, she said to the young nuns who were trying to keep her at home, "Mes enfants, let us do our duty, and leave the doctors to do theirs!"

And now, what are we to gather from all this?

I must leave it to your own judgment. You want to do right, and with God's help you will be able to see the proper limits of that "reasonable service," which elevates him who commands, honours him who obeys, seeks before all things the will of God, and respects the claims of the soul, while taking into consideration the requirements of the body.

PATIENCE.

"After these things was a festival day of the Jews, and Jesus went up to Jerusalem.

"Now there is at Jerusalem a pond, called Probatica, which in Hebrew is named Bethsaida, having five porches.

"In these lay a great multitude of sick, of blind, of lame, of withered, waiting for the moving of the water.

"And an angel of the Lord descended at certain times into the pond: and the water was moved,

And he that went down first into the pond after
the motion of the water, was made whole of whatsoever infirmity he lay under.

"And there was a certain man there, that had
been eight and thirty years under his infirmity.

" Him when Jesus had seen lying, and knew that
he had been now a long time, He saith to him,
Wilt thou be made whole ?

" The infirm man answered him, Sir, I have no
man, when the water is troubled, to put me into the
pond. For whilst I am coming, another man goeth
down before me.

" Jesus saith to him, Arise, take up thy bed, and
walk.

" And immediately the man was made whole :
and he took up his bed and walked. And it was
the Sabbath that day." *

I wish I could persuade those poor invalids who
have been vainly hoping for recovery during many
a long year to take heart and profit by the example
of the poor paralytic.

For more than thirty years this poor man had
been deprived of the use of his limbs, and had come
day after day to the pond of Bethsaida, never losing
his trust in God's help ; sorely tried, but always
victorious through his unshaken confidence. At
the hour when the angel " troubled the water," as
the Evangelist tells us, he tried to plunge into the

* St. John v. 1-9.

healing bath, but some less feeble sufferer had
always been before him. Yet he never lost hope
and courage.

One day that his faith brought him to the pond
as usual, and he had again missed the longed-for
chance, he lay down beside the water in uncom-
plaining patience, when suddenly he saw near him
a Man with a graver and more gentle aspect than
other men, and from whose lips proceeded those
strange words, " Wilt thou be made whole ? "

Must not the question have sounded like a cruel
mockery to the poor paralytic, after eight and
thirty years of disappointed waiting ?

" Sir," he meekly answers, " I have no man, when
the water is troubled, to put me into the pond.
For whilst I am coming, another man goeth down
before me." Jesus saith to him, " Arise, take up
thy bed, and walk."

Marvellous words ! and in their effect still more
wonderful. In one moment the Saviour rewarded
the long patience of His servant.

" Arise and walk ! " My brother, you too will
one day hear those words of resurrection and life,
but they will only come at the hour known to God,
and you must learn to await them in patience.

It is the way of God's providence not to accomplish in a moment His greatest works, but to follow
the laws and requirements of time in His government of the world.

If the paralytic man had been cured in the beginning of his illness, he would not have edified others and advanced the glory of God by offering the spectacle of a soul full of life and of enduring patience, in a body already half-dead. But help comes at last, for the Friend of our souls will never "suffer us to be tempted above our strength." His Hand is suddenly put forth, when succour is no longer expected. So sudden and speedy is our relief, that we are astonished at our own happiness. Such are the ways of God's love.

Oh, how blessed is that hour, how full of consolation and happiness, when the presence of the Divine Friend is restored to the soul, and with it all the effects of His Almighty compassion! Blessed, above all, when it has been purchased by long days of unshaken patience, and when the unlooked-for help comes to crown a hope which has never failed! What greater proof of faith and love can the soul give to her God, than patient endurance such as this? Can any other proof be so convincing, as hope, which no persistent science can shake, and faith, which no banishment can stagger?

Christian soul, this is a great work to which I am now exhorting you. The holy writer of the "Imitation" is struck with its magnitude, whilst he is recommending it. "It is much, and very much, to be able to forego all comfort, both human and divine, and to be willing to bear this interior banishment for God's honour."

Sickness adds still more to the trials of this banishment; and the sick and desolate Christian who is steadfast in faith, and hope, and love, even whilst he seems to himself to be forsaken of God, is in truth a martyr, and one of those salutary victims who are offered up as whole burnt-offerings, in union with the all-atoning sacrifice of Christ.

Christian soul, who read these pages, if prolonged suffering has so wearied you as to dim faith and love in your soul, close this book for a while, and tell your Heavenly Friend that, should such be His blessed will, you are ready to continue suffering for his greater glory.

Lie down with the poor paralytic beside the pond. Look on without any feelings of anger or envy whilst others descend into its healing wave and come forth made whole. Murmur neither against God nor man, but wait patiently for Him Who is coming to you, for I tell you He will come at last.

"A little while," said the Saviour, "and you shall not see Me; and again, a little while, and you shall see Me." *

" For yet a little, and a very little while, and He that is to come will come, and will not delay." †

* St. John xvi. 16.   † Heb. x. 37.

READING.

If sickness does not incapacitate you for all mental exertion, so that you are still able to occupy yourself with reading, be thankful for this help, and take good care to profit by it. To say nothing of the harm which mental depression does the soul, we may be sure that it acts injuriously upon the body, whilst a wise and moderate degree of intellectual exertion tends to quicken and sustain physical life.

Let us suppose that your sickness, though it does not leave you strength enough for your ordinary occupations, still allows you the comfort of such reading as will not put too much strain upon the mind. What books will you choose? Have you been hitherto of the number of those who, while very careful in selecting their friends, are not at all particular in the matter of books, and become familiar with many whose authors they would blush to associate with? There are people who fall into this gross inconsistency, and live habitually, notwithstanding their professions of religion, in the intimacy of writers of corrupt minds, or of at least doubtful morality.

The season of sickness is a fitting time to dismiss such dangerous visitors. Brought low, as you are, by that physical weakness which reacts upon the soul, beware of giving yourself up unarmed to the attacks of temptation!

The invalid has to live much on his own thoughts. Memory is the constant companion of long hours of wakefulness and loneliness. Let this companionship be pure and ennobling; do not suffer its tone to be lowered, lest it bring you the sting of unwelcome recollections, instead of being a source of purifying consolation. Virginal purity is memory's fairest treasure; happy they who have never lost it, for once lost, no regrets, no strivings to forget, can restore the ruin.

I am quite of opinion that you should read amusing books; for it is highly desirable for you to avoid *ennui* and low spirits, and to keep up your courage by that cheerful temper which enlivens heroism itself, and is good company even to the soldier on the battle-field. Your bed of sickness is a field of battle, and I would remind you of the proverb, "Contre mauvaise fortune, bon cœur."

But choose well the books which are to cheer and amuse you. Choose what is simple, natural, and full of ennobling interests. Avoid those romantic and sensational works in which the author has striven after a laboured and complicated plot, the great object being apparently to do away with all traces of probability or common sense. Wretched books, whose aim is not to touch the soul, but the senses and nerves of the reader, and whose only effect is to leave him in a state of

feverish excitement.   This is not precisely what
you are in want of just now.

But if sensational novels are poison to the
weakened imagination of an invalid, those pro-
ductions of late years, which, under the title of
realism, have done so much to lower and vitiate
the minds of many amongst us, are equally to be
dreaded.   Never open one.

Really good books, books that are amusing,
clever, refined, and instructive as well as amusing,
are not, thank goodness, so rare.   Select these, and I
will answer for it that their society will be a source
of intellectual profit to you, and a real solace.

But, my friend, there is another kind of reading
to which God more especially wishes you to turn
your mind.   It may be that in the bustle of
your ordinary occupation you have found little
leisure for that serious reading which is profitable
to the soul ; you should, therefore, gladly take
advantage of the opportunity which now offers
itself, of listening a while to the voice of God and
of His saints.

What books shall I recommend to you for
spiritual reading?   What does our holy mother,
the Church, recommend to her children ?

First, there is the Book of books, the Scriptures.
It may be that you have arrived at your present
time of life without having read the New Testament, without, that is, having read it with such a

thorough reading as you are ready enough to bestow on any literary production which pleases you. If this be true, I regret it for your own sake. You have perhaps become acquainted with the portions of this blessed Book which are read during Mass on Sundays, and have imagined that in this way you gained sufficient knowledge of its divine contents. This is a grievous mistake; you may not discover it till you reach old age, and find yourself a prey to that spiritual weakness which comes from never having studied the Gospel.

Your sickness will be an inestimable blessing if it only makes you well acquainted with this most holy Book. Open it at the first page, and read on. Do not trouble yourself about the divisions of chapters and verses; read as long as you feel inclined. You will be surprised to find how the interest of this reading suits itself to the state of your mind. It is the property of God's works, that they seem to be made specially for each one of us, as well as for all in general. Nothing is easier to understand, more varied in meaning, more soothing, and at the same time grander and more full of power, than this divine Book. Jesus Christ is not here described by the hand of man; He Himself reveals Himself to us; it is from His own adorable Lips that those blessed words fall which, for nineteen centuries, have had power to dry tears and soothe every suffering.

You will find the Acts of the Apostles very cheering; they show us how God has been pleased to make use of human frailty and nothingness to accomplish His greatest works.

If you are in great suffering, read the Acts of the Martyrs; they are full of examples which will both instruct and encourage you. In those pages you will read of the joy of self-sacrifice; of victories gained over the weakness of the flesh; of death, met face to face, and shorn of all its terrors in the light of this unshrinking gaze. Above all, you will learn from these histories of primitive ages the high price which God sets upon the sufferings of His children, and the tender love with which He gathers up their tears. You will be ashamed to complain of your own trials, when you come to see the labours of the Martyrs, and you will blush for your cowardice when you hear the heroic utterances of little children and tender virgins in the midst of torture.

Read the Lives of the Saints. They are God's work in man; they tell of the wonderful power of grace, which is here shown forth in an endless variety of ages and characters.

I may also recommend to you several of St. Jerome's letters, that are full of comfort and encouragement; also some of the letters of St. Augustine, as well as this great saint's Confessions, and his commentaries on certain of the Psalms more especially the 136th, " Upon the rivers of Babylon." In this last, the weariness of this world's trials, even when borne without murmuring or despondency, and the longing of the Christian for his heavenly home, are expressed in language which has rarely been equalled by any human pen.

I need hardly remind you of the " Imitation of Christ." Its author was a man deeply versed in spiritual science, and wrote, at a period of great and general calamity, for those souls who sought to leave exterior for interior things, as the mystics were wont to express it. There is a tradition respecting this book, that whoever opens it at random is certain to light upon something peculiarly applicable to his present need.

The works of St. François de Sales are also admirably adapted to the season of sorrow and suffering.

The teaching they contain is holy, vigorous, and profound, clothed at the same time in attractive language, so that we shall find ourselves at once interested and even amused by their perusal.

I may mention, further, the minor works of Bossuet, especially his discourse on "Abandonment to the Will of God," the one on " Life hidden with God," and his reflections on the " Agony of our Blessed Lord ;" also an admirable work of Pascal's, which is too little known, on the " Right Use of Sickness."

Christian sufferer, these and such as these are the books which I would have you read. Jesus says to you now, as the Apostle did to his dearly beloved Timothy, "Till I come, attend unto reading." * " *Till I come.*" These words are full of mystery, if we interpret them of Him Who is ever coming to us. Christ comes to us in our sorrows and in our joys ; He comes in increasing trials, as well as in relief and comfort; He comes in the healing of our bodies in this world, as well as in the everlasting salvation of His children in the life to come. In whatever way He may vouchsafe to visit you, wait for Him, suffering soul. Wait for Him, in watchfulness, in prayer, in holy meditation, and pious readings.

" Till I come attend unto reading."

Attende lectione dum venio.

VISITORS.

The first thing you have to do now, is to close your door ; the second is, to know to whom you should open it. If it be advisable that a sick man's library should be formed with care, with what carefulness and caution ought he not to choose his company ! Visitors ! Be careful about these living books that you cannot always dismiss at will, and who will sometimes keep on talking to you, when

* 1 Tim. iv. 13.

you are worn out with weariness and longing to drop asleep!

We agreed at the beginning of this book that amongst the chief spiritual benefits to be derived from sickness, are retirement, silence, and self-recollection. God would have you be silent, and the physician gives you the same advice; here, then, at any rate, is a case in which both the heavenly and the earthly authorities are at one. It would surely be inexcusable for you to disobey them. There is so much talking in the world, and you yourself have talked so much during the last ten years, say, that a silent interval of a few days might really be a rest to your soul. You say that you are fond of novelty; leave off talking for a while: who knows but you may discover in the experiment new sensations which will surprise you!

I am now speaking of silence with regard to conversations, friends, and visitors. Silence is, in the first place, the visit of God to the soul, and I would remind you once again to consecrate the largest, calmest, and best part of your time to this heavenly guest. Let your visitors be few in number. First on the list are those whom God's providence has appointed for you, those who are around you and wait upon you—your near relations, your servants. No effort is necessary to receive these; you make no attempt with them to seem lively, or amused, or anything but what you are.

N

Believe me, it is worth while to enjoy such a rest as this from the strain of keeping up appearances. Receive gladly the loving ministrations of those who wait upon you, and see that you pay them back largely in gratitude and love. All the flatteries which the world is so ready to give you in abundance when you are in no need of help are not worth a straw compared to the care of a faithful servant, whose self-devotion is only known to yourself.

After your immediate family circle, welcome with joy and thankfulness a small number of intimate friends, if God has blessed you with such. These will know how to choose the most suitable times for their visits ; they will pray with you, or read to you, or enliven you with their conversation. The more you suffer, the more they will cling to you ; the more weary and dreary your sick-room becomes, the oftener they will cross its threshold ; their friendship will increase in proportion as your need of it increases, and if there should come a day when it is dangerous to approach you, some of them will brave even this, and forget their own safety to soothe your sufferings.

As to other visitors, who else would you include? If you mean a certain select few, who, though not very intimate, still take a real interest in your state, and do not come merely as a matter of heartless formality, I would say, admit them by all means.

See, however, that you do not weary them with sighs and complaints, but let them see that a Christian knows how to bear his trials.

If, over and above these, you mean by visitors those worldly-minded people who gad about from house to house, full of hollow condolences, of false comfort, of worldly maxims and interested attentions; gossips, who waste time in backbiting, and trying to cure incurable *ennui ;* heartless actors of which there are so many on this world's stage—if you mean visitors of this class, I can but advise you to keep your door inexorably closed against them.

But, alas ! I am talking all this time of the danger and inconvenience of having too much of this world's favour, as if I were addressing myself solely to the prosperous ones of the earth, to those who are loaded with worldly blessings, and satiated by their very abundance. But I am not forgetting Christ's dear and suffering servant, who lies in his wretched garret, parched with fever, and longing for the coming of some charitable visitor. He needs no warning against the dangers of too much company; he is not troubled with over many friends ; no worldly-minded bores come knocking at his door.

No need to impress on you, my poor brother, the duty of gratitude. When, after a long, lonely night, and a day, perhaps, as long and as lonely, some friend, whom God's loving-kindness has sent, stands by your bedside, your feverish hand holds

his with a welcome which no money can buy, and
when he leaves you, your eyes follow him, full of
grateful tears, which God records to your account.

Oh! yes, my poor brother, receive thankfully these
visitors sent to you by the God of love; prize them,
and hold them very dear. They, at any rate, will
bring you no hollow professions or hypocritical
compliments; you may safely believe what the messenger of charity says to you, for he would not be
standing there unless he loved you, and felt for
you.

Receive, then, with gratitude the young man of
wealth and position who comes quietly into your
little room, and slips his offering under your
pillow.

Welcome the delicate, fine lady, who sits down
by your bedside; accept her loving services, for to
seek your company she has forsaken the rich and
happy ones of this world.

And as for us who are loaded with this world's
goods, let us blush when we think of our manifold
blessings, and of our manifold abuses of them, and
let us pray God to restore to our souls that which
the world is daily striving to take from us, namely,
simplicity, humble gratitude, and the power of dis-
cerning true riches.

RUINS.

Diseases, which we may call the assaults of death, sometimes leave in our bodily frame a general languor, or some particular infirmity, or the first marks of old age; or, it may be, deformity or ugliness. It is only of the last of these ruins that I am now going to speak.

Ugliness! What shall we say of this affliction, which, though the one that is oftenest to be met with in the world, is yet the one that men look upon with the greatest contempt, as if all men, more or less, sooner or later, were not marked with its brand? It has been said that, "If there existed a race of men who were immortal, the idea of death would be more terrible to them than it is to us." *

Might we not say, If there existed a race of men who were perfect in beauty, they would be more indulgent to ugliness than we are? But every one is more or less ugly, and every one is severe on the ugliness of others.

What a proof this is of our want of charity and of our stupidity!

What words can we find, even the most compassionate of us, to soothe this trial which is all the more grievous because of a certain touch of ridicule which attaches to it? What can we say to those sorely afflicted ones, whose features are disfigured,

* Count X. de Maistre.

or whose limbs are maimed by the wounds and deformities caused by disease, or by the remedies which have removed it? How can we comfort those disinherited ones who are driven to hide themselves from the gaze of their fellow-men, who shrink from the kindest eyes, hardly daring even to show themselves in the house of God during the hours of service, and whose one desire is to escape observation and hide themselves away in some corner where they may live and die unseen. God alone, Jesus Christ alone, and He crucified, can comfort these. He can and He will. But His hand alone is tender enough to touch your wounds without adding to their pain. My brother, turn aside from men. Forget their heartless scorn, and cling to Jesus, the Comforter for all who are in sorrow and stricken with infirmity.

But, O my God, what is this that I behold? O Blessed Jesus, "art Thou not beautiful above the sons of men?"* Art Thou not He whom children loved, and to whose arms they gladly came—they who ever seek whatsoever is lovely? Art Thou not He whom of whose beauty the spouse in the Canticle of Canticles sang in prophetic rapture? Whence comes it, then, that even Thy prophets seem hardly to recognize Thee? Whence comes it that shame and sorrow have set their marks upon Thine adorable face? The prophet

* Psalm xliv. 3.

Isaias sees Thee, by the eye of faith, through the vista of far-off ages ; he beholds Thee climbing the sacred mount, fainting beneath the burden of the cross, and yet he declares that he knows Thee not.

"Who hath believed our report ? and to whom is the arm of the Lord revealed ?

" And He shall grow up as a tender plant before Him, and as a root out of a thirsty ground : there is no beauty in Him, nor comeliness : and we have seen him, and there was no sightliness, that we should be desirous of Him.

" Despised, and the most abject of men, a man of sorrows, and acquainted with infirmity : and His look was as it were hidden and despised, whereupon we esteemed Him not.

" Surely he hath borne our infirmities, and carried our sorrows : and we have thought Him as it were a leper, and as one struck by God and afflicted.

"But He was wounded for our infirmities, He was bruised for our sins : the chastisement of our peace was upon Him, and by His bruises we are healed."

O King, crowned with insult and reproach, Thy prophet at once expresses and explains the mystery. It was to heal my stripes that Thou wast stricken ; it was to raise me from the depths of my humiliation that Thou didst vouchsafe to be covered with shame and confusion. Yet I have dared to murmur, O my God !

The slights of men have been to me a heavier burden than I could bear, and the bitter marks of their scorn have raised a storm of angry feelings in my heart. But I look upon Thee, O Jesus; I hear Thy words, as Thou sayest to me, Behold, My son, and compare the reproaches thou endurest with those I bore for thee. "But I am a worm, and no man : the reproach of men, and the outcast of the people. . . . They have dug My hands and feet. They have numbered all My bones.

"And they have looked and stared upon Me. They parted My garments amongst them; and upon My vesture they cast lots.

"All they that saw Me have laughed Me to scorn : they have spoken with the lips, and wagged the head." *

I hear Thy voice, O Lord : I will unite my sufferings with Thine. I will no longer murmur, but take refuge in silence ; I will forget the scorn of men, I will forgive and accept it ; nay, more, I will love and welcome it, since it has rested on my Saviour's brow, before it fell on mine.

O Word of God, Brightness of Eternal Beauty, Thy brightness was hidden, dimmed, tarnished for love of us ; Thy beauty was marred by the anguish of Thy Passion, and by Thy death upon the Cross. I adore Thee, O Lord ; I love Thee, in Thine abasement. I unite my deformity to the blows

* Psalm xxi. 7, 18, 19, 8.

and spits from which Thou didst not hide Thy face. I unite the stains which the chastisement of sin has left on my body with those sacred marks which love has impressed on Thine. I would hide myself with Thee in the reproach of the Cross in this world, so that I may one day appear with Thee, changed into Thy likeness.

"It is sown in dishonour; it shall rise in glory."[*]

IMAGINARY AILMENTS.

You have probably amongst your acquaintances met people who have never known what it is to be really ill, but who are ready to complain whenever they can get up the slightest ailment, under the impression that a certain well-bred languor is becoming and interesting. If any passing agitation disturbs their sleep for a night, they will tell you they suffer from continual wakefulness, and are burnt up with fever. If a little nervous fatigue gives them a headache, they shut themselves up, and lie on the sofa, talk of their sufferings, and insist on being waited on, and nursed, and made a fuss over. They grumble, and give trouble, and perhaps cry, to help to pass the time; they are out of spirits without knowing why; they think themselves ill used by everybody, so they worry

[*] I Cor. xv. 43.

everybody ; they complain that life goes hardly with them, and declare that they are enduring horrible, atrocious pain.   If they feel the least physical uneasiness, they will send for their medical man, thus taking up for the relief of a mere imaginary ailment the skill and attendance for which many real sufferers are waiting.   If, taking pity on their supposed ills, you inquire what really is the matter with them, they will tell you that they are suffering martyrdom.   Do not swell the ranks of such martyrs.

I advise you, my friend, not to be so morbidly watchful over your health as to let every passing ailment upset your nerves and put a check to all exertion ; neither must you imitate that singular affectation which seems to take delight in every little indisposition, to boast of it, to make much of it, and parade it on every possible occasion.

People sometimes carry this mania to such an extent, that at last they become really ill, and end by turning their whimsical fancies into actual sufferings.   It would almost seem, in such a case, as if God's providence had fulfilled their wishes by giving them what they appeared to seek, namely, really delicate health to take care of and brood over.   We all know that idle, rich people, surrounded as they are by every luxury, occasionally invent new maladies of which the hardworking poor do not even know the names, and succeed in creating for themselves real pains and infirmities out of fancied ailments.

Do not be so skilful in the art of self-torture ; reserve your complainings and your heroism for the real trials which are sure to come sooner or later, and do not draw too largely on the pity of your friends before the time when you will really need it. There is great danger in pretences of this sort. They are lowering to the soul, which is held back by them from active, earnest work ; they are a mockery to the real misfortunes of our fellow-creatures, and they are a provocation to the justice of God, Who hates the affected murmurs of thankless prosperity.

SICKNESS IN EXILE.

You have fallen ill, here in your own country, in your own home, in the midst of those who love you and surround you with tender care, and yet you complain, and perhaps accuse God's providence.

Have you ever thought of the traveller, a prey to sickness far away from his own country, in some inn, where he hears only a foreign language, where he sees only indifferent or greedy faces ?

Have you ever thought of the passenger who is left, sick, at the first port where his ship touches, hundreds of miles from the country for which he was bound ; who, from a foreign soil, watches the sails of the vessel as they vanish below the horizon, bearing away his last hope of ever again seeing his native land?

Have you thought of the young wife who leaves her father and mother, to follow her husband to far-off lands, and having watched his dying bed, has to finish her journey alone, and to land alone, in a strange country in the first hour of her sorrow?

Have you thought of the exile who longs to see his mother once more before he dies, but feels himself sinking fast, and knows that a foreign grave will close over him?

Have you ever thought of the poor sailor stricken with deadly sickness, lying in the ship's hospital, which is only four feet in height, and there nursed by some kind-hearted but unskilful messmate, while he gazes with sad forebodings on the watery winding-sheet which has enfolded so many before him?

Have you thought of the missionary whose strength fails him, and who lies down in the midst of the jungle, exhausted with fatigue and broken down by fever, whilst his native attendant goes away in search of succour?

Have you thought of the Sister of Mercy, who sets out joyously, and by-and-by falls a victim to her heroic labours in some distant land?

Have you thought of the young soldier who sinks down on the line of march, struck by the fire of the enemy, or the ravages of pestilence, and sees his regiment, his comrades, his friends, pass him by, loses sight at once of his colours and his country, and dies, after hours of suffering, in a hastily constructed camp hospital, under a burning Indian sky?

My brother, I am not setting before your eyes an imaginary picture. These are realities which are to be met with every day, almost every hour ; we cannot look round the world without coming across them.

Weak and cowardly as we are, shall we dare to complain of our own small trials, when we compare them with trials like these?

TWO HOMES.

At the beginning of winter, when the first snows lay on the ground, a poor man and a rich man fell ill. They lived not far from one another. When the rich man felt the touch of sickness on him, he remained within doors, retired to his comfortable room, sent for the doctor, and at once every precaution was taken.

The poor man rose feeling ill, but he went to his work as usual to earn the daily bread.

The rich man was never left alone. The fever declared itself, but loving care and the best skill of the city watched by his pillow. His wife and children never left his room, and vied with each other in rendering him every little service he required.

The poor man came home that first day from his work, giddy with pain and burning with fever. It was dark, and he staggered painfully up the steep stairs that led to his garret, pushed open the door, and found no one within, and no comforts but a straw mattress and a fireless hearth.

But the rich man complained. This illness would upset his plans, and interfere with his business. He foresaw entertainments, too, which he should be obliged to postpone, opportunities of gaining distinction which he should miss, important occupations which would be suddenly broken in upon; he counted up the loss which he would be likely to sustain through his inability to attend to business. All these complaints he poured into the ears of his wife, who tried gently to turn his thoughts to other subjects.

When the poor man had stretched himself upon his miserable pallet in the dark, he soon heard footsteps coming up the staircase, and then some one entered the room, and lighted a candle. His three little children and his wife came to his bed-side, and the poor woman murmured as she looked at him, "Alas! you are going to be thrown out of work; and meantime where shall we find bread?"

The rich man was kind-hearted and charitable.

He sent for his steward, and gave orders that a sum of money should be distributed to the poor, thinking rightly that these alms would plead in his behalf before God.

The poor man beheld his wife tired out with her hard day's work. The little ones were clinging to their mother. He could not speak, but through his dizzy brain floated that ever-present dread of the poor—hunger!

He foresaw in a moment what the poor man fears when sickness comes upon him : an empty grate, his children crying for bread, his credit gone, his place in the workshop filled up, and, in case his illness lasted, notice to quit from his landlord, his little stock of furniture pawned or sold, and finally the workhouse or the hospital.

Medical men were called in to attend on the rich man. The most eminent skill and care were exhausted in his behalf.

The poor man's wife was obliged to give up her work ; she sent for the parish doctor, and applied for parish relief. She was questioned, told her case should be taken into consideration, and sent away. The doctor came the next day ; he was kind and skilful, but tremendously overworked ; he remained a few minutes in the miserable little room, and then hurried away ; for he had on his list fifteen more poor patients to be visited before the end of his round.

The rich man's illness ran its course ; but, thanks
to the skill and the devoted attention which surrounded him, no dangerous symptoms appeared ;
a certain amount of anxiety was the sharpest trial
which had as yet crossed the threshold of the
luxurious home.

By this time the poor man was reduced to great
distress, and having parted with the last few relics
remaining to him of his parents and the days of
his childhood, he had nothing more left to sell, and
knew not where to turn for help.

A financial scheme presented itself to the rich
man ; his agent and his lawyer consulted together,
and determined not to trouble him about the
matter in his present state of health ; but three
of his friends came forward, and advanced the
money which was requisite.

The wife of the poor man dressed herself as
neatly as the wretched remnants of her clothes
would allow, and went to the house of one of her
neighbours whom she knew to be in easy circumstances, and implored him to lend her a few shillings.
This neighbour was good-natured.   Taking the
shillings from his purse, before all his household,
he held forth on the thoughtlessness of the poor, on
their want of foresight, their imprudence, their fail-
ings of various kinds, declaring that with industry
people could always get on, and that economy,
cheerfulness, and patience were indispensable to

the labouring classes. Then he solemnly handed over to her the money, and recorded the debt in his account-book.

And so things went on for some time ; the rich man growing a little better, and the poor man a little worse, though the latter was kept, day by day, from utter starvation by the kindness of Christian charity. When spring came, and the sun shone once more on the budding leaves and flowers, the rich man was convalescent, and ordered away to his country seat, that change of air might bring back his strength. These orders he promptly obeyed, and then went to drink the waters of a famous healing spring in the South of Europe, where he remained during the winter, as a matter of precaution.

But, with the summer days, fresh troubles came upon the poor man. One by one, the friends who had helped him went out of town, and he was left alone. The rent of his room was in arrear, and his worst forebodings on the night when he was taken ill came to be fulfilled. He received notice to quit ; his few remaining sticks of furniture were sold ; then came the workhouse, a bed in the hospital, and in a month he was dead.

On the day of the poor man's death, the rich man wrote to one of his friends :—"You would hardly believe, my dear friend, how many annoyances, perplexities, and difficulties of all kinds my unfortunate illness of last winter has caused me. Since that time everything has gone wrong. I had to let several most advantageous affairs slip through my hands, and to leave uncompleted a first-class speculation in which I had embarked ; I could not stir from the fireside all last winter, and here I am now in a foreign country, away from my business and all I take pleasure in ! I try to resign myself to the will of Providence, but I confess that I find it hard to do this, and I cannot help envying those who are in a humble walk of life, and free from the cares of business, and who have no important interests at stake. The more I think of it, the more I am convinced that these people are very much mistaken when they complain of their lot, and that in reality they are much better off than we are."

Reader, are you quite sure that neither you nor I ever wrote that letter ?

THE GRACE OF CONSOLATION.

The Sick Man. Lord, the day wears on and the sun already begins to decline : Thy words and Thy grace have sustained me until this hour, but fresh trials come with mid-day, and, as it were, fuller floods of suffering. I see the business of life going on all around me, I hear far-off sounds which speak to me of the diligent and useful labours of my fellow-creatures. Suffering and weakness compel me to live a selfish life, just as pleasure causes selfishness in others. This thought fills me with sorrow and humiliation, for, O my God, Thou didst give me a heart to love Thee, and a will to work for Thy glory and the good of my fellow-creatures.

Why am I, then, so powerless, while longing to do Thee service, or why do spiritual love and longing outlive the strength to exert them? Lord, quench this holy fire which burns to no purpose in my heart, and only makes still heavier the burden of a useless life.

The Comforter. Has the initiation of suffering taught thee nothing, O My child? Listen to My words, and lay them to heart. Of all the things which man must learn, the most hidden and mysterious is suffering. However tender a man's heart may be, or however quick his instinct, he will never understand the sufferings of others, unless he himself has suffered ; he will speak of them as a blind man might talk of colours. Hence the common incapacity of those who have never known suffering to console those who suffer. Nothing can make amends for this want; not the warmest affection, not the most entire devotion.

Personal experience can alone break down the barrier, and give us the grace of consolation for others.

Hast thou not often felt this, My child? What

comfort hast thou met with in thine hours of weakness from those gay and prosperous people on whom fortune has smiled uninterruptedly? Many of them loved thee well, and earnestly desired to help thee; but wise and kindly as their words might be, that word was always wanting which would have brought thee comfort. This mysterious word, this drop of holy unction, nothing can teach it to the soul but a personal acquaintance with suffering.

This law is so deep and so universal, that even I, Who am possessed of all knowledge, I willed to feel every secret of human misery in the weakness of the flesh, that so I might become to man that experienced Comforter whom he so greatly needs in time of distress. My participation in their sorrows draws men powerfully to Me; and when the fire of trial comes upon them, it is not to the contemplation of My glory on Mount Thabor that they turn, but to My Cross on Calvary. There, seeing in My sacred Limbs the furrows of their own afflictions, they say with unshaken confidence, " For we have not a High Priest who cannot have compassion on our infirmities ; but one tempted in all things like as we are, without sin." *

This science of suffering is so important that nothing can make up for the want of it. He who has it not, let him beware how he attempts to deal

* Heb. iv. 15.

with the sorrows of others ; but he who possesses it may do all things, for he bears within himself a healing power.

He who has suffered, who has passed through long years of grief and affliction, of wearing anxiety, of secret heart-sinkings, of disappointed hopes and lonely tears—such a one, if he has not received his soul in vain, ought henceforward to pass through the world as a living sacrament of My consolation. Such a one cannot fail to have a soothing influence on suffering souls. The sick, the sorrowful, the afflicted, recognize him at once from amongst other men. Others may speak, but he only holds the secret of that watchword, which finds its way to the stricken heart, and acts like balm upon its wounds.

Such a one is gentle, tender, patient towards pain. He knows that a sick man has become a child again, and that if he needs bracing words to stir up the dormant energies of his mind, on the other hand, his weakness requires the indulgent ease and watchfulness of a mother. He who has himself been taught by suffering has the art of gently turning sick souls to thoughts of Me. He will not, as some do, make his zeal a pretext for a harshness which of itself provokes and excites opposition. "The bruised reed He shall not break, and the smoking flax He shall not quench." *

Therefore rejoice, O My child, that thou hast

* Isa. xlii. 3.

known what it is to suffer, and be comforted that
thou art still called upon to suffer; this initiation
into suffering is an unspeakable treasure. Thou
wilt soon seek out the afflicted; or, if thou canst
not go in search of them, they will come to thee.
Welcome the sorrowful as sent to thee by Me;
welcome them as those for whom thou hast learnt,
and laboured, and suffered; welcome them as
those I have committed to thy care in this world.
Thou wilt need no studied words wherewith to
speak to them; open thy heart and show them the
scars of thine own wounds; tell them that thou
hast known what it is to suffer; listen to the story
of their trials, and answer them out of the fulness
of thy heart. Rich in this treasure of consolation,
thou mayest go without fear amongst the poor and
sorrowful. Thy griefs will disappear before their
griefs, thy sufferings will vanish before their sufferings; thou wilt forget thyself in ministering to
others, and when evening comes round, thou wilt
be surprised to feel a new life springing up within
thee; and thou wilt say to Me in thy thankfulness,
" Lord, what is this that has befallen me ? Whither
hast Thou been leading me, and what have I done ?
I know not how it has happened, but whilst I have
been striving to do for others, it seems as if I had
in reality been doing all for myself; in trying to
heal them, I have been healing my own wounds;
in seeking to console the afflicted, I have dried my

own tears ; in endeavouring to calm their griefs, I have lost the bitterness of my own ; in giving the little that I had, I have found all."

EVENING.—THE HOUR OF LONELINESS.

There is one hour for the invalid harder to bear than even the time of his first waking. This is the last hour of the day, when evening ends and night begins. Throughout the day, he has been in a measure consoled for his own inaction by the society and attentions of those around him. Friends meet by his bed, seeking to amuse him ; they read to him, they entertain him, and do all they can to turn his thoughts from his trials. But as the night closes in, these helps are withdrawn, and the sufferer is left alone.

Most of us know the dreariness of that time, when the thoughtful nurse, having done all that kindness can suggest, withdraws for the night, and leaves us to the society of a flickering lamp, with the prospect of many long sleepless hours before us. This time of repose for the rest of the world, is for the sick man a season of misery and restlessness. More fatigued by long inaction than by the hardest work, he can find no rest nor refreshment ; the small remains of strength which are still left to him only add to his sufferings, a feverish excitement takes possession of him, and troubles his soul.

What can I say to you, O suffering Christian, to lighten the burden of this weary trial? What memory shall I invoke to comfort you in this hour of your passion?

In this utmost extremity of distress and anguish, I know of but one help in the world, one last but never-failing help—the sacred Passion of the Saviour. The Eternal Word of God could have redeemed the world by a single command from His adorable lips; think you, then, that it was without a special purpose that He vouchsafed to descend to the weakness of our mortal nature, and to experience the extremest pains which that nature is capable of sustaining? Such a work as this must surely reveal some great purpose. The Saviour willed not only to redeem His elect from eternal death, but also to comfort them, to strengthen them, to support them during their life in this world, and to transfigure every earthly pang, by leaving upon it the impress of His patience and His victory.

What has He, then, done for the special relief of the sick in their evening solitude? Verily, He Himself knew and passed through this hour, and illuminated it to all ages with the light of a solemn and blessed memory.

Let us open the Gospel. "Then Jesus came with them into a country place which is called Gethsemani; and he said to His disciples, Sit you here, till I go yonder and pray.

"And taking with Him Peter and the two sons of Zebedee, He began to grow sorrowful and to be sad.

"Then saith He to them, My soul is sorrowful, even unto death : stay you here, and watch with Me.

"And going a little further, he fell upon His face, praying, and saying, My Father, if it be possible, let this chalice pass from Me. Nevertheless not as I will, but as Thou wilt.

"And He cometh to His disciples ; and findeth them asleep, and He saith to Peter, What? could you not watch one hour with Me?

"Watch ye, and pray, that ye enter not into temptation. The spirit indeed is willing, but the flesh weak.

"Again the second time, He went and prayed, saying, My Father, if this chalice may not pass away but I must drink it, Thy will be done.

"And He cometh again, and findeth them sleeping : for their eyes were heavy.

"And leaving them He went again : and He prayed the third time, saying the self-same word."*

Until the hour of night in which His passion really began, our Blessed Lord was surrounded by His disciples. He partook with them of the Last Supper, He left them the divine testament of His Body and His Blood, He gave them His last

* St. Matt. xxvi. 36–44.

counsels, He prayed for them. But the hour of the Sacrifice draws nigh, and this Sacrifice begins in solitude. Jesus enters into the Garden of Gethsemani; there He separates Himself from the greater number of His apostles; but, as if shrinking from utter isolation at the time of His great agony, He keeps with Him the best-loved ones, those who had seen His glory on Mount Thabor— St. Peter and the two sons of Zebedee. To them He discovers the secrets of His soul, to them He reveals the immensity of His sadness, and seeks the support of their sympathy and their prayers.

He is alone! He now experiences all the terrors and the anguish and shrinkings which solitude adds to suffering. He falls into that agony in which a bloody sweat testifies to the extremity of what He is undergoing. Twice, sorrowful even unto death, He returns to His chosen friends, seeking help and sympathy from them, and twice He finds them asleep. He again leaves them, and returns to His solitary prayer.

Poor sufferer, left alone for the night, troubled by gloomy forebodings and cruel phantoms, it was for you that our Lord passed through that hour of darkness and desolation in the Garden of Gethsemani. The world has forsaken you, and is busied even at this moment with its pleasures and its gaieties; the echo of its joys perhaps reaches you on your bed of suffering. Let it pass. Envy

not the intoxicating draught of its false happiness ;
but unite your separation from it to the parting of
Jesus from His disciples at the entrance of the
garden.

By-and-by your relations, your dearest friends,
your most faithful servants, leave you in their turn;
it is not that they are unfeeling or unfaithful, but
they are weak, like all who are weighed down with
the burden of the flesh, and weariness will make
itself felt, in spite of love. " Their eyes were heavy."
Do not grudge them the rest which their service
through the day has earned ; do not ask them to
watch with you any longer; do not let their
slumber irritate you ; be strong against your own
weakness. Take heart ! Learn to bear being left
alone, and unite this second desertion to the loneliness of Jesus, when He left His three disciples,
and went alone to drink the bitter cup of His
agony. If, however, overcome by suffering and
the anguish of loneliness, you do awaken one of
your nurses, and ask her to help you, do not be
vexed if you see her stupefied by fatigue, hardly
able to answer you, serving you hurriedly, and
falling back at once into sleep. Do not feel
aggrieved, or reproach her, or harbour unjust
thoughts. Peter, James, and John loved their
Divine Master, and yet they slept the sleep of
human weakness beneath the olive trees of Gethsemani. Keep silence once more, and unite this

third loneliness, which is the hardest of all to bear, to that of Jesus, when He left the three disciples to their slumbers. Terrors, mental misery, sadness beyond your power of control, may overtake you ; unite them to the extremity of sorrow which caused our Blessed Lord to fall on His face to the earth. If you weep, let it be with Jesus, for He wept ; if you complain, let it be with Jesus, for He complained ; if you pray for deliverance, let it be with Jesus, for He prayed to be delivered ; but ask as He asked, saying, " Father, if it be possible, let this chalice pass from Me. Nevertheless not as I will, but as Thou wilt."

Be with Jesus, be alone with Him. And this means, O Christian soul, that you will never be alone ; for your Divine Friend, Who is always with you and always watchful to help you, will send to you the angel of His secret and salutary consolation.

"And there appeared to Him an angel from heaven, strengthening Him."

NIGHT.

My brother, see that you do not murmur too loudly against the night for the sleeplessness and restlessness it brings you. Reverence the night, on the contrary, and count it sacred, for it has often been the chosen hour of God.

It was at night that she who bore the Saviour of

the world left her lowly home with St. Joseph, in obedience to the decree of Cæsar, and journeyed along the roads of Judea to Bethlehem. It was at night that she knocked at the doors of many dwellings there, and was sent away from all, and found no room even in the inn. It was at night that the angels sang, in the brightness of a dazzling light, "Glory to God in the highest, and on earth peace, good will towards men;" and it was at night that the Holy Child was born. It was at night that the angel of the Lord warned St. Joseph, and that this faithful servant of God rose up, and "took the Child and His mother," and fled with them from the sword of Herod, and went into Egypt.

It was at night that Jesus was awoke by the cry of His disciples, "Lord, save us, or we perish," and that, "rising up, He rebuked the wind, and said to the sea, Peace, be still. And the wind ceased: there was made a great calm."

It was at night that Nicodemus came to Jesus, and that the Master took compassion on the weakness of His poor servant, and taught him the doctrine of regeneration. It was at night that the same Divine Teacher, gathering His faithful ones around Him, ate with them His last Supper, and gave them His Holy Body for food, and His Blood for drink.

It was at night that Joseph of Arimathea, and the other faithful followers, wrapped the Lord's body "in linen clothes with the spices," and that the Pharisees made the sepulchre sure by setting a watch.

It was at night that Peter was awakened in the prison by the angel of the Lord, and that thinking he saw a vision he was delivered from his chains, and following the angel, found himself free. It was at night that the angel appeared to Paul in bonds at Jerusalem, and said, "Be constant : for as thou hast testified of Me in Jerusalem, so must thou bear witness also at Rome."

It was at night that the Christians of the primitive Church were wont to bear to the catacombs the precious remains of the martyrs, and hastily to engrave a palm-branch on the stone which covered them.

It is at night that penance weeps, that charity watches, that the sick man suffers most. It is at night that God's angel, passing over a great city, sees the brave self-conquest of some poor tempted girl side by side with the dark orgies of sin, and spares the guilty city for the sake of that one righteous soul.

Meditate on these things as you lie sleepless, ye suffering ones. Lift up your hands by night, and praise the Lord, and the darkness of night shall be brighter than the day to you, and night itself will be illuminated with light and joy.

"And night shall be light as the day : the

darkness thereof and the light thereof are alike to Thee." * "In the time of the evening there shall be light." †

THE CRUCIFIX.

Lord, the hour of desolation came upon me, and I knew not how to bear it. All the powers of my soul quailed beneath the burden of a bitterness greater than I could endure. In the time of this terrible anguish I sought for help ; I looked round me, thinking that so much suffering must needs call forth some comforter ; but no comfort appeared.

Then I bethought me of Thine image, O Christ Jesus. I laid hold of it with a trembling hand, and bowed my tear-stained face upon it. Oh! it is good to weep upon Thy Cross, my crucified Lord, as those who have so wept know well. Through my tears I gazed upon Thy blessed hands, pierced for the love of sinners ; I embraced Thy sacred feet, nailed for us to the cruel tree ; my hand sought the wound in Thy precious side. I felt very close to Thee, as I kissed Thy life-giving wounds, and looked upon Thy thorn-crowned head.

From the bottom of my soul there arose that cry which Thou, O Jesus, didst pronounce in Thy last agony, "Father, into Thy hands I commend my spirit." I dwelt on these precious words till their

* Psalm cxxxviii. 12.   † Zech. xiv. 7.

meaning seemed to penetrate my whole soul. I wept, but my tears were not bitter as before, and instead of the angry murmurings which had filled my soul, there arose to my lips an involuntary strain of thanksgiving. I felt that my weak will had been steeped seven times in the blood of the Lamb.

Why must these moments of rapturous peace pass away? Why is it not granted to us to die while they last?

Oh, Cross of my Saviour, never let me forget Thy precious consolations, Thy power against the promptings of despair, and Thy sweetness which changes tears into peace.

Oh, dear Saviour, may it be granted to me to fix my dying eyes upon Thy Cross; may some friendly hand place it then within my hands, lift it before my eyes, press it to my lips. If, in that solemn hour of death, I am too weak to pray, grant that Thy presence may still thus be brought close to me. Happy shall I be if I may so die beneath the shadow of the Cross, in the light of Thy loving look, like thy servant who on his death-bed fixed his eyes on the crucifix, murmuring, " I can no longer pray to Him, but I can look at Him."*

* The last words of Père Lacordaire.

THE DELAYS OF GOD.

The acute pangs of suffering are not the only trials we have to bear. These may be short-lived, passing away after they have racked the body for a time. Far more grievous is that long-continued pain which goes on from day to day, and with a monotony that nothing seems materially to increase or lessen. This continuous suffering, without any prospect of change, throws the soul into a state which is neither despair nor impatience, but a sort of disgust of suffering. The soul sinks under the crushing weight of the same unending trials. She has only strength to say to God, "How long wilt Thou forget me, O Lord? unto the end? How long dost Thou turn away Thy face from me?" *

A soul thus weighed down often loses all clear-sightedness; she looks for nothing from the future, she thinks no change possible in her lot. This is an ordinary effect of very prolonged sufferings. All that now remains is, for the soul to now rise to the extraordinary effort of hoping against hope.

When the storm has lasted long, and the sky is black with clouds; when, as far as the sailor's eye can reach, he sees nothing but the angry crests of the waves, and the surge of the mighty billows, it seems to him as if he were never more to see the

* Psalm xii. I.

P

sun, as if the storm-tossed ocean would never again sink to rest. And yet a change in the wind is enough to sweep away the clouds, and suddenly turn the roaring sea to a quiet lake.

Christian soul, you can never hope enough! What you take to be God's forgetfulness is, in reality, the effect of His love. He delays, it is true, but He acts thus towards those whom He loves, and from whom He expects great deeds to His glory. Let us look once more into the Gospel, for no one can comfort you so well as Jesus, by His own blessed words and works. Let us be silent, then, and read.

"Now there was a certain man sick, named Lazarus, of Bethania, of the town of Mary and of Martha her sister.

"(And Mary was she that anointed the Lord with ointment, and wiped His feet with her hair: whose brother Lazarus was sick.)

"His sisters therefore sent to Him, saying, Lord, behold, he whom Thou lovest is sick.

"And Jesus hearing it, said to them, This sickness is not unto death, but for the glory of God: that the Son of God may be glorified by it.

"Now Jesus loved Martha, and her sister Mary, and Lazarus.

"When He had heard, therefore, that he was sick, He still remained in the same place two days.

"Then after that He said to His disciples, Let us go into Judea again.

"The disciples say to Him, Rabbi, the Jews but now sought to stone Thee: and goest Thou thither again?

"Jesus answered, Are there not twelve hours of the day?

"If a man walk in the day, he stumbleth not, because he seeth the light of this world:

"But if he walk in the night, he stumbleth, because the light is not in him.

"These things He said: and after that He said to them, Lazarus our friend sleepeth: but I go that I may awake him out of sleep.

"His disciples therefore said, Lord, if he sleep he shall do well.

"But Jesus spoke of his death: and they thought that He spoke of the repose of sleep.

"Then, therefore, Jesus said to them plainly, Lazarus is dead.

"And I am glad for your sake that I was not there, that you may believe: but let us go to him.

"Thomas therefore, who is called Didymus, said to his fellow-disciples, Let us go also, that we may die with Him.

"So Jesus came and found that he had been four days already in the grave.

"(Now Bethania was near Jerusalem, about fifteen furlongs off.)

"And many of the Jews were come to Martha and Mary, to comfort them concerning their brother.

"Martha, therefore, as soon as she heard that Jesus was come, went to meet Him : but Mary sat at home.

"Martha therefore said to Jesus, Lord, if Thou hadst been here, my brother had not died :

"But now also I know that whatsoever Thou wilt ask of God, God will give it Thee.

"Jesus saith to her, Thy brother shall rise again.

"Martha saith to Him, I know that he shall rise again in the resurrection at the last day.

"Jesus said to her, I am the resurrection and the life : he that believeth in me, although he be dead, shall live.

"And every one that liveth, and believeth in Me, shall not die for ever. Believest thou this ?

"She saith to Him, Yea, Lord, I have believed that Thou art Christ, the Son of the living God, Who art come into this world.

"And when she had said these things, she went and called her sister Mary secretly, saying, The Master is come, and calleth for thee.

"She, as soon as she heard this, riseth quickly and cometh to Him.

"For Jesus was not yet come into the town : but He was still in that place where Martha had met Him.

"The Jews, therefore, who were with her in the house, and comforted her, when they saw Mary that she rose up speedily and went out, followed her, saying, She goeth to the grave to weep there.

"When Mary, therefore, was come where Jesus was, seeing Him, she fell down at His feet, and saith to Him, Lord, if Thou hadst been here, my brother had not died.

"When, therefore, Jesus saw her weeping, and the Jews that were come with her weeping, groaned in the spirit, and troubled Himself,

"And said, Where have you laid him?

"They say to Him, Lord, come and see.

"And Jesus wept.

"The Jews, therefore, said, Behold how He loved him.

"But some of them said, Could not He that opened the eyes of the man born blind, have caused that this man should not die?

"Jesus, therefore, again groaning in Himself, cometh to the sepulchre. Now it was a cave, and a stone was laid over it.

"Jesus saith, Take away the stone. Martha, the sister of him that was dead, saith to Him, Lord, by this time he stinketh; for he is now of four days.

"Jesus saith to her, Did I not say to thee, that if thou wilt believe, thou shalt see the glory of God?

"They took, therefore, the stone away: and Jesus, lifting up His eyes, said, Father, I give Thee thanks that Thou hast heard Me.

"And I knew that Thou hearest Me always; but because of the people, who stand about, have I said it; that they may believe that Thou hast sent Me.

"When He had said these things, He cried with a loud voice, Lazarus, come forth.

"And presently he that hath been dead came forth, bound feet and hands with winding-bands, and his face was bound about with a napkin. Jesus said to them, Loose him, and let him go." *

Let us read this Gospel over and over, and then kiss the blessed page, and thank God with all our hearts for having ordained that these things should be recorded for the never-ending comfort of mankind. And yet there are some surprising details in this Gospel narrative; for it is said that Jesus, when He had heard that Lazarus was sick, abode two days still in the same place where He was; and Lazarus dying during the space of these two days, Jesus said to His disciples, " Lazarus is dead. I am glad for your sakes that I was not there." Lastly, when Jesus came to the sepulchre and said, "Take away the stone," Martha answered, "Lord, he is now of four days." O Saviour, Thou didst love Lazarus with a tender love; why, then, didst

* St. John xi. 1–44.

Thou delay two whole days before going to his aid. Why didst Thou not heal him at the beginning of his sickness? Why, lastly, didst Thou wait four days before restoring to Thy friends, Martha and Mary, the brother who was so dear to them?

Such are the mysteries of Thy delays, O Lord. But one of Thy sayings sufficiently explains them to us, " This sickness is not unto death, but that the Son of God may be glorified by it." Whether, therefore, we consider Thy glory, the honour of Thy friend Lazarus, the welfare of the Jewish multitude, and of mankind in all succeeding ages of the world, nay, even the joy and happiness of the two loving sisters whom Thou Thyself didst love—in all these we see plainly that each delay in the workings of Thy mighty power was but an effect of Thy wisdom and Thy love.

For if Lazarus had been cured in the beginning of his sickness, he would not have been the same wonderful and enduring witness to the divinity of the Gospel, nor have testified through the centuries against the heresies of the unbeliever by the great fact of his resurrection.

Had Lazarus been cured in the beginning of his sickness, he would not have been the blessed witness of the ineffable tenderness of our Saviour shedding tears at the tomb of a friend, and the Jews would not have said, in speaking of those tears of God for a man, " Behold how He loved him."

Had Lazarus been cured in the beginning of his sickness, he would not himself have known the depths of the love of his Divine Friend ; he would not have realized how this love equals and surpasses the powers of death.

Had Lazarus been cured in the beginning, there would not have been the same rapturous happiness in the house at Bethania, as when he came back from the dark recesses of the sepulchre, and pressed to his heart once more Martha and her sister Mary.

Marvellous delays of the Saviour ! Mysterious tarryings, little understood of men ! Their shortsighted affection is too ready to doubt and mistrust Thy dealings, for man has but a little time to love ; whilst endless ages wait at Thy bidding, O Christ, and Thou dost choose from amongst them Thine own hour in which to pour out joys and consolations on those who have waited for Thee.

Christian soul, wearied and overwhelmed by the long night of sufferings, do not confound the mysterious delays of God with forgetfulness. Even if you should seem to be, like Lazarus, already gone down into the tomb ; if the most skilful physicians should have condemned you to death, thus in a manner sealing beforehand the stone upon your tomb ; if you should have to say with Job, " My flesh is clothed with rottenness and the filth of dust," * do not give up hope, you may yet

* Job vii. 5.

hear the footsteps of Him Who comes when most
unlooked for. At the sound of His life-giving
voice your "heart" and "flesh shall rejoice in the
living God:"* you may still, if so He wills, break
your bonds, and, casting off your grave-clothes,
come forth, leaning like Lazarus on the Everlasting
Arms ; you may once more return to life. But your
return will be something like that of one who has
already passed the gates of death, and they who
see it will give glory to God.

The Prayers of the Gospel.

My brother, do not be over-troubled because of
your weakness in God's sight, but be resigned when
you cannot pray to Him as you wish, for He knows
your infirmities, and records the very least of your
endeavours to serve Him. Besides, have you ever
considered the sort of prayers our Blessed Lord
vouchsafes to hear and answer in the Gospel?
They are so very simple that the greatest weakness
could hardly hinder you from making use of them.

A leper comes to Jesus and says, "Lord, if Thou
wilt, Thou canst make me clean," and Jesus answers
quickly, " I will ; be thou made clean." †

A centurion comes and says, " Lord, my servant
lieth at home sick of the palsy, and grievously

* Psalm lxxxiii. 2.   † S. Matt. viii. 2, 3.

tormented." "I will come and heal him," answers
our Lord. The centurion adds, it is true, those
beautiful words which have ever since been the
petition of those who draw near to God's altar:
"Lord, I am not worthy that Thou shouldst enter
under my roof; but only say the word and my
servant shall be healed." *

The disciples are in a ship with Jesus on the
Lake of Gennesareth; the wind rises, the waves
roar; the disciples are terrified, and cry out, "Lord,
save us; we perish." Immediately Jesus commanded the winds, and the sea, and there came a
great calm.†

A poor woman who had had an issue of blood
for twelve years, came behind Him and touched
the hem of His garment. She did not even venture
to speak to Him; the Gospel tells us that she
only said within herself, "If I shall touch only
the hem of His garment, I shall be healed." But
Jesus, turning and seeing her, said, "Be of good
heart, daughter; thy faith hath made thee whole."‡

Two blind men cry out, "Have mercy on us, O
Son of David." Jesus saith to them, "Do you
believe that I can do this unto you?" They say to
him, "Yea, Lord." Then He touched their eyes,
saying, "According to your faith, be it done unto
you." And their eyes were opened.§

---

* St. Matt. viii. 6–8. † St. Matt. viii. 24–26.
‡ St. Matt. ix. 20–22. § St. Matt. ix. 27–29.

A woman of Canaan comes to Him, and says, "Have mercy on me, O Lord, Thou Son of David : my daughter is grievously troubled by a devil." At first the Saviour seems not to hear her, but she draws nearer and falls on her knees, saying only, "Lord, help me." Jesus wishes to try her faith. He says, "It is not good to take the bread of the children and to cast it to the dogs." But she said, "Yea, Lord, for the whelps also eat of the crumbs that fall from the table of their masters." Then Jesus answering, said to her, "O woman, great is thy faith : be it done to thee as thou wilt." *

A wealthy Jew, named Jairus, came to Jesus, saying, "My daughter is at the point of death ; come, lay Thy hand upon her, that she may be safe and may live." Jesus rises immediately and follows the ruler towards his house ; but as they draw near the house, some of the friends of Jairus met them, and said to the father, "Thy daughter is dead : why dost thou trouble the Master any further?" But Jesus, having heard the word that was spoken, saith to the ruler of the synagogue, "Fear not, only believe." He entereth in where the damsel was lying. And taking the damsel by the hand He saith to her, "Damsel, I say to thee, arise." And immediately the damsel rose up, and walked.†

One day, a poor paralytic, hindered from draw-

* St. Matt. xv. 22-28.   † St. Mark v. 22-42.

ing near to the Saviour by the multitude which filled the house where He was, caused himself to be let down through the roof. This single proof of his great faith and hope stood him in the stead of any prayer, and before he had opened his mouth, Jesus said to him, " Man, thy sins are forgiven thee ; " and directly afterwards, " Arise, take up thy bed, and go into thy house." *

On another occasion, a mother's silent tears obtained all they asked for. The Saviour was entering the little town of Nain, and met at the gate the funeral procession of a young man whom they were carrying to his grave ; following the bier was the widowed mother, whom, when the Lord had seen, being moved with mercy toward her, He said to her, " Weep not." And He came near, and touched the bier. And He said, " Young man, I say to thee, arise." And he that was dead sat up, and began to speak. And He gave him to his mother.†

The public sinner of the city also spoke only by her tears. She knew that Jesus was in the Pharisee's house ; she went in silently, and standing at His feet began to pour ointment on them, to wash them with her tears, to wipe them with her hair, to cover them with her kisses. Those around were surprised and offended at the sight : " This man, if He were a prophet, would surely know who

* St. Luke v. 18–24.　　　　† St. Luke vii. 11-15.

and what manner of woman this is that toucheth Him, that she is a sinner." But Jesus defends her : " Wherefore I say unto thee, many sins are forgiven her, because she hath loved much." And to herself He said, "Thy faith hath made thee safe ; go in peace." *

Neither did Zacheus speak ; it was his alacrity which drew down upon him his Saviour's blessing. From the top of his sycamore tree, whence he watched the Lord pass by, he heard these words of everlasting comfort : " Zacheus, make haste, and come down ; for this day I must abide in thy house." †

Listen, again, to the words of the mother of the Saviour at Cana. " They have no wine," she said. Wonderful simplicity of the prayer of Mary's heart, and wonderful its efficacy, for our Saviour's first miracle was wrought in answer to it.‡

Silence pleads for the woman taken in adultery ; she remains silent before our Lord, whilst her accusers heap upon her reproaches but too well deserved. It would almost seem as if she did not dare to raise her guilty voice to the ear of the All-Holy One, and so she remains dumb, crouching before Him in the consciousness of her own vileness and shame. This silence touches the heart of Jesus. He looks at her accusers and says, " He

* St. Luke vii. 36–50. † St. Luke xix. 2–5.
‡ St. John ii. 1–10.

that is without sin among you, let him first cast a
stone at her." They all shrink away, one by one,
and Jesus is left alone with the sinful woman. He
said, "Woman, where are they that accused thee?
Hath no man condemned thee?" She said, "No
man, Lord." And Jesus said, "Neither will I condemn thee. Go, and now sin no more." *

What can be simpler and shorter, and yet more
efficacious, than the prayer of the two disciples at
Emmaus? Jesus made as if He would go further,
but they say unto Him, "Stay with us, because it
is towards evening, and the day is now far spent,"†
and the Saviour grants their request. He tarries
with them, and makes Himself known to them in
the breaking of bread.

Have you sufficiently dwelt upon and penetrated
yourself with that beautiful Gospel of Lazarus that
we have read together? What wonderful simplicity
and yet what reality they display! A few short
sentences, a cry from the depths of the soul; and
yet how marvellous the answer which they drew
from our Saviour!

First of all they sent unto Him, saying, "Lord,
behold, he whom Thou lovest is sick." After receiving this message, Jesus resolves to return to
Jerusalem. "The Jews but now sought to stone
Thee," says His disciples: "and goest thou thither
again?" But this hinders not our Lord's merciful

---

* St. John viii. 3-11.   † St. Luke xxiv. 28-35.

purpose ; he whom He loveth is sick, so He rises up and goes to help him. When Martha hears that the Saviour has come, she hastens to meet Him. " Lord," she exclaims, " if Thou hadst been here, my brother had not died ! " A few moments after, Mary also comes, and, falling at the feet of Jesus, she has only strength to repeat Martha's words : " Lord, if Thou hadst been here, my brother had not died ? " The Son of God does not turn a deaf ear to this cry of love and sorrow. Jesus, therefore, when he saw her weeping, troubled himself, and said, " Where have you laid him ? " They say to him, " Lord, come and see." Then Jesus wept.*

O tears of my Saviour ! I love, and bless, and thank Thee for these precious treasures. They are a divine justification of the tears we shed over those we have loved and lost, but still more are they an adorable proof of Thy love for man, and of Thine ever ready sympathy with his sorrows.

A prayer was addressed to our Blessed Lord during the last moments of His life. A poor thief hanging on his cross, close to the Cross of Jesus, has faith enough during his dying agonies to turn to the Saviour and say, " Lord, remember me when Thou shalt come into Thy kingdom." He was the last human being to whom the Son of God spoke before " He gave up the ghost," and to him were

* St. John xi. 1–35.

spoken these merciful and loving words, "Amen I say to thee, this day thou shalt be with Me in paradise." *

Such are the prayers the memory of which our Lord has been pleased to treasure up for us in the Gospel.

O heart of man which God hath made, and of which He sees and knows both the strength and the weakness, if you suffer, tell out your suffering simply to your eternal Friend Who loves you, and will enter into all your griefs. Make no attempt at fine language ; all you need is to show Him your tears, that He may wipe them away and comfort you. Be not troubled that you have no other words than a confession of your own weakness, like the lispings of a sick child upon its mother's knee.

O Jesus, Who dost love a simple prayer, and art pleased in Thy Gospel forthwith to answer petitions offered up in this spirit of childlike simplicity, grant to us who kneel before Thee that we, too, may pray with childlike hearts, that we may forget ourselves, and think only of Thy compassion, Thy tenderness, and the sympathizing tears which Thou didst weep over the griefs and sufferings of mankind.

* St. Luke xxiii. 42, 43.

MIRACLES.

My brother, be not like unto those Jews and Greeks, of whom St. Paul speaks when he says, "The Jews require signs, and the Greeks seek after wisdom." * Be not of the number of those who are so blinded by the light of their own arrogant reasoning, that they refuse to believe even what they see, and deny the miracles of God which surround them. On the other hand, be not of those who refuse to believe unless they " see signs and wonders," and who are too carnal-minded to take pleasure in the unfailing spectacle of God's providential government of the world; who are always asking for wonders, and will not believe that God loves them unless He works miracles in their behalf.

Be rather like those wise and simple souls who look upon God as a Father, all-loving and all-powerful, who believe firmly that He can, if it so pleases Him, work a miracle for them, though in their humility they rarely ask for one, and never without adding that prayer of prayers, " Father, Thy will be done." Souls such as those often hear the divine answer, "Go in peace; thy faith hath made thee safe."

Suffering Christian, when human science has

* 1 Cor. i. 22.

Q

failed to relieve you, if you are led by the strong
promptings of faith to invoke the omnipotence of
God, and to ask some visible and extraordinary aid
at His hands, do not let your hopes be quenched
by the sophisms of the wise ones of this world. Let
not your faith be weakened by that profane reasoning which nowadays assails us on all sides ; hold
fast to your belief in God, notwithstanding the
sneers of the Greeks. Believe that God can work
a miracle for you if He so wills it, and that, in
thus believing, you are guided by sound and true
reason. "The spiritual man," says St. Paul,
"judgeth all things."*   Let us examine and
judge.

Do you believe in the divine personality? In
other words, do you believe that God is a living
Person, wise, loving, able to feel for you, to understand your needs, to pity your sufferings, to love
you, and to help you?   Undoubtedly you do ; for
if God is not all this, He is not at all, and we know
that He is.

Do you believe that this personal God has created
the world, and governs it; that everything has come
from Him, and that He upholds all things by His
power?   Do you believe, as a necessary consequence, that all the forces of nature belong to
Him, and that He can make use of them according
to the good pleasure of His eternal wisdom?   Yes,

* 1 Cor. ii. 15.

undoubtedly; for if God has not created the world, He is not at all, and we know that God is.

Do you believe that this personal and creative God is free to work out His own designs? Do you not believe that, in laying down the general laws which govern the universe, He remained free to lay down exceptions to those laws without contradicting His own wisdom? Do you not believe, moreover, that the first of the general laws which rule the world is this law of divine liberty, and that this sovereign independence, far from being, as in the case of human authority, an occasion of caprice, is, on the contrary, the foundation of an infinitely wise and unchanging might? Yes, undoubtedly; for if God is not free amongst His own creatures, God is not at all, and we know that God is.

A personal, wise, loving, good, powerful Creator of the world, Ruler of all created things, Author of the laws which govern the universe, as well as of the exceptions to those laws, free amongst His own works—this God *can* work miracles; and if He can do it, He does it, for with God no power remains unexercised.

Thus far reason. Now let us turn to the Gospel. Everything here shows us the same God in mortal flesh, face to face with our ills, curing our sicknesses, healing our wounds, delivering our bodies from pain and decay, from loathsome and cruel infirmities,

nay, even from death itself after its reign has
begun.   What Jerusalem saw with bodily eyes,
and handled with the hands of flesh, all the world
has since then seen and felt.   Every land has re-
echoed the cry of adoration which for three years
resounded along the shores of Gennesareth ; all
human woes have been lightened or cured by the
all-powerful gentleness of Jesus, whilst those who
groaned under them have been converted to the
God of Lazarus.   For now nearly two thousand
years, when the sufferings of men are more than
they can bear, the sufferers turn to Christ.

Trust, then, O my brother, this infallible instinct
of suffering humanity ; accept this blessed tradition
by which, for nineteen hundred years, man, de-
spairing of help from his fellow-men, has turned to
God.   Believe the testimony of those two unchanging witnesses, suffering and death, both of which
declare to you that they know but one conqueror,
Jesus, the Son of David and the Son of God.

If your sufferings threaten to be more than your
strength will bear, throw yourself with the leper,
with the centurion, with the paralytic at the pool,
with Martha and Mary—throw yourself, with all
these, at the feet of Him Who is never weary of
healing the infirmities of all mankind.   Resign
yourself beforehand to accept whatever may be
the Divine will, and then ask all, believe all, hope
all, knowing that, if the Jews eighteen hundred

years ago saw and felt miracles, others amongst ourselves have also seen and felt them, and are at this very time bearing a joyous testimony to the almighty power of the Saviour of mankind.

If, then, led by strong faith, you should venture to ask a miracle, remember to seek it with humble submission, saying, as Jesus has taught us, "Father, Thy will be done. But not what I will, but what Thou wilt." For if the haughty unbelief of the Greeks affronts God's omnipotence, not less does the exacting presumption of the Jews insult His wisdom.

What shall we say of these earthly-minded souls who, when they seek a miracle at God's hands, stake their faith on the obtaining of it, and are so shaken if they are not answered according to their expectations, as to give way to doubts and murmurs. O weak souls! Weaker even in reason than in faith, and unworthy to bear the glorious name of Christian! Ignorant, too, as well as proud, who thus dare to pronounce judgment on the doings of God! Why do they distrust His providence? Is it not because He has not seen fit to alter on their behalf the accustomed order of the universe?

I can find no excuse for you, O carnal souls, and with fear and trembling I pronounce upon you these words of the Saviour, "A perverse and adulterous generation seeketh after a sign, and no sign shall be given unto it." Perverse, in that you care little for God's glory in the miracle, and only seek your own advantage. Adulterous, because at the least delay of the Divine Spouse you are ready to turn from Him to strangers. It is hardly worth while to be a Christian, if your worship of God's providence is to be so low and mean as this. If the faith of Christians were no other than this presumptuous confidence which demands that God should overthrow the course of the world for the sake of our private interests, and makes us fly out in rebellious murmuring when our wishes are not granted, then verily the philosophy of the Stoics were preferable, and Marcus Aurelius and Epictetus, with their reverence for the mysteries of the divine government of the world, were wiser and more enlightened than we.

But who believes this? Who can confound the confiding trust of faith with the insolent presumption, or the embittered disappointments of superstition? Woe unto us, if we so abuse the unspeakable love of our God, as to become familiar and exacting towards His compassionate majesty, and claim miracles at His hands as if we were exacting the payment of a debt! Woe unto us, if our close and constant experience of the divine goodness lessens our reverence and adoration for God's awful majesty and wisdom! It is at once a certain and exalted principle that governs the world by the simplest means and the most general laws. This steadiness of the general laws of God's providence is one of its greatest glories, and such a plain token of His wisdom, that St. Augustine does not hesitate to call it a more striking testimony to His glory than any miracle ; he adds that signs and wonders are only given to man in order to awaken his attention, which is apt to slumber, surfeited by the spectacle of the regular order of the universe.

It is easy for us to praise the course of God's providence when it meets our own wishes. To most men the best of all possible worlds is that in which they are happy—that which ministers to their passions, contents their ambition, and provides them with honours and pleasures ; but the thanksgiving of such men is manifestly too selfish to find acceptance with Heaven. The righteous man who suffers, and who, though tried by long reverses, still does not cease to adore the wisdom of God without asking for a miracle of which he feels himself to be unworthy, or without murmuring if the miracle which he asks for is not granted, does real honour to God, and offers up holy and acceptable praise. The Christian who is thus at once filled with fortitude and resignation, does not share in the childish delusion of those optimists who think there can be nothing better than this world. He knows very well that this world is not, since sin entered it, what God first made it ; but he also knows that this world is not, since Jesus Christ came into it, what sin had made it. He knows that in Christ Jesus "all things work together unto good," * and that if we cannot love trials and sufferings in themselves, we can at least accept them, and even love them by looking at them as the will of God, Who permits them in His love, which alike sanctifies and rewards them.

Try, my brother, to be a Christian like this, wise in your faith, reverent and humble in your prayers. If, urged by a holy trust in God, you have asked of Him some extraordinary aid, and your prayer is granted, give thanks, and, without taking to yourself any of the honour which belongs to Him alone, go and proclaim His glory. If your prayer is not granted, take refuge in patience, in courageous and humble love, in silent adoration of the divine wisdom ; your Father knows better than you what you need. In all things, and above all things, love God ; love His providence, love the holy order of His laws, love the mercy with which He overrules evil, believe without hesitation that He can always work the greatest miracles ; but do not lightly tempt His power and His wisdom ; believe and love under prolonged trials, as well as in the comfort of relief ; be, in fact, a worshipper "in spirit and in truth," that so you may one day see Him Whom

* Rom. viii. 28.

you have waited for unfalteringly through the mystery of faith and patience.

"Blessed," says our Lord, "are they that have not seen, and have believed." * They shall see Heaven, that miracle of love which will never pass away.

THE RETURN TO LIFE.

My child, it is not for thyself that thou hast received again the gift of life. This newly given life belongs to thy fellow-men ; it is to be used in their service and to My glory. If thou wouldst know to whom amongst men thou dost owe thy life, I answer thee, to all mankind. Thy ambition must not be narrowed to labouring in this world for the good of those souls who are placed near thee. A Christian's interests should be universal ; nothing should be indifferent to him which concerns My glory. It is his duty and his right to care for all that goes on throughout the world. All his life long he is continually breathing this prayer, "Father, Thy kingdom come, Thy will be done on earth as it is in heaven." And what does this mean, but that a Christian must be constantly watching over the earth and praying for it ?

My Apostle understood this when he said to the Christians of his own time, " I desire, therefore, first

* St. John xx. 29.

of all that supplications, prayers, intercessions, and thanksgivings be made for all men;"* and also when, in the largeness of his heart embracing the whole world, he exclaimed, "Who is weak, and I am not weak? Who is scandalized, and I am not on fire?" declaring that, besides all the sufferings and persecutions which he had borne, there was also upon him "the solicitude for all the Churches;"† solicitude, that is, for all souls all over the world.

These things, My son, are true of all Christians. There is, indeed, a difference in the particular application of these universal precepts to different states of life, but there ought to be in the soul of every Christian a deep and apostolical longing for the salvation of the world. Death, whose near approach thou hast so lately felt, is often the messenger whom I send to remind my children of this their vocation. Death extends the circle of man's thoughts, aspirations, wishes, and affections. It shows suddenly, with a vivid light, the simple reality of all things; all that is temporal disappears, and the soul sees nothing but the salvation of the world and God's presence.

Such, My child, is the message of death to the soul.

Blessed are the souls who, having received it, bear it in mind ever after.

This feeling of universal sympathy for the joys

* 1 Tim. ii. 1.   † 2 Cor. xi. 28, 29.

and sorrows of all men, with a view to My glory, will not hinder thee from fulfilling thine own particular duties ; it will not awaken in thy soul any foolish distaste for the narrow round of thy daily task. Thou wilt not be like those dreamers, who, though in theory they are always labouring for the welfare of the human race, die at last without having rendered the smallest real service to one of the lowest of their fellow-men. This guilty sorrow will not be thine; for thou wilt remember that, however narrow and obscure the nature and extent of the labour allotted to thee, in performing well that labour thou art effectually helping to forward My great designs. Thou wilt be thus both humble, and eager for My glory, and full of boundless and ardent aspirations for the advent of My kingdom amongst men.

Thus, My son, wherever thou mayest be, however contemptible thy lot in the eyes of men, thou wilt be one of My true servants, one of those who from the beginning have laboured with Me for the salvation of the world. Let, then, this noble ambition take possession of thy soul ; say no longer, " I will save myself," say rather, " I will save the world."

Begin by suffering. O My child, it is by suffering that mankind is saved. Of all the latent powers which conduce to the salvation of the world, none is so powerful as suffering sanctified by union with My Cross. Hast thou still to learn that a soul raised above itself by true love for God has many calls to suffer?

See what disorders there are amongst men! What forgetfulness of God! What profanation of His holy Name! What worldliness amongst the good! What crimes amongst the wicked! What cause for tears on all sides! Behold all this and suffer—suffer and pray, and wait, and strive.

Lastly, remember that thou hast passed through the very jaws of death, and that such a deliverance should not be received in vain. Cast from thee, therefore, once and for ever, that personal, narrow, selfish life, from which I have roused thee by the touch of suffering, and learn to say with My Apostle, "Whether we live, we live under the Lord; or whether we die, we die unto the Lord. Therefore, whether we live or die, we are the Lord's."

THE END.

PRINTED BY WILLIAM CLOWES AND SONS, LIMITED,
LONDON AND BECCLES.

www.ingramcontent.com/pod-product-compliance
Lightning Source LLC
Chambersburg PA
CBHW020103030726
47498CB00006B/1930